Readers Love An

A Heart Without Borders

"I felt like I was right there with the characters, feeling the heat, the desperation and the total devastation right along with them. There is no doubt in my mind that this book will stay with me for a long time."

—The Novel Approach

"In true Andrew Grey fashion, this book delivers not only a romance but a powerful lesson on the courage, hope and optimism of people in a country devastated by disaster and poverty."

—Hearts on Fire Reviews

Stranded

"A great story of how time passes and people allow their relationship to settle into routine and they lose their appreciation for their partner. This doesn't mean that they are no longer deeply in love, sometimes they just need a reminder."

—Gay List Book Reviews

"*Stranded* is an amazing combination between an intense thriller-like stalker story, a sizzling romance, and a character study which, through tension and drama, brings out the worst and the best in both main characters."

—Rainbow Book Reviews

A Daring Ride

"All the things we've come to love from Grey are there in the print. An emotional, engrossing, and sexy ride is what's in store with this latest work from one of the best authors in the genre."

—MM Good Book Reviews

"I quickly got sucked in by the story and the characters. There really is so much substance in the plot and the people… he doesn't need a lot of extra language to pull you in."

—Mrs. Condit & Friends Read Books

Readers Love Andrew Grey

An Isolated Range

"Mr. Grey delivers a highly emotional story that captures the reader's heart in one fell swoop. This is an author who is dedicated to his series, stories and characters. With each range story, you always find yourself drawn in, breathless until the very last page is read."

—Dawn's Reading Nook

"Andrew Grey's Range series just gets stronger with each new book and *An Isolated Range* is perhaps the most amazing addition yet."

—Scattered Thoughts and Rogue Words

"*An Isolated Range* is a story not of human triumphs but also of sadness and death. This is an author who balances both so well that the reader is left speechless after that last page is read."

—Love Romances and More

The Fight Within

"I loved this book, these characters, and this story. Get it today. Read. Understand and through understanding, enjoy."

—Mrs. Condit & Friends Read Books

"This is a story that is rich in detail, delving into the Native American culture and also sharing the suffering that the Native American's still face today."

—MM Good Book Reviews

"This was a very powerful read."

—Live your Life, Buy the Book

Novels by ANDREW GREY

Accompanied by a Waltz
Dutch Treat
A Heart Without Borders
In Search of a Story
Inside Out
Stranded • Taken
Three Fates (anthology)
Work Me Out (anthology)

ART SERIES
Legal Artistry • Artistic Appeal • Artistic Pursuits • Legal Tender

BOTTLED UP STORIES
Bottled Up • Uncorked • The Best Revenge • An Unexpected Vintage

THE BULLRIDERS
A Daring Ride • A Wild Ride

CHILDREN OF BACCHUS STORIES
Children of Bacchus • Thursday's Child • Child of Joy

GOOD FIGHT SERIES
The Good Fight • The Fight Within • The Fight for Identity

LOVE MEANS… SERIES
Love Means… No Shame • Love Means… Courage • Love Means… No
Boundaries
Love Means… Freedom • Love Means … No Fear
Love Means… Family • Love Means… Renewal • Love Means… No Limits

SENSES STORIES
Love Comes Silently • Love Comes in Darkness

SEVEN DAYS STORIES
Seven Days • Unconditional Love

STORIES FROM THE RANGE
A Shared Range • A Troubled Range • An Unsettled Range
A Foreign Range • An Isolated Range• A Volatile Range

TASTE OF LOVE STORIES
A Taste of Love • A Serving of Love • A Helping of Love • A Slice of Love

Published by DREAMSPINNER PRESS
http://www.dreamspinnerpress.com

Novellas by ANDREW GREY

A Present in Swaddling Clothes
Biochemistry • Organic Chemistry
Shared Revelations
Snowbound in Nowhere
Whipped Cream

FIRE SERIES
Redemption by Fire • Strengthened by Fire • Burnished by Fire • Heat Under Fire

CHILDREN OF BACCHUS STORIES
Spring Reassurance • Winter Love

LOVE MEANS… SERIES
Love Means… Healing • Love Means… Renewal

WORK OUT SERIES
Spot Me • Pump Me Up • Core Training • Crunch Time
Positive Resistance • Personal Training • Cardio Conditioning

Published by DREAMSPINNER PRESS
http://www.dreamspinnerpress.com

Robyn
Hugs & Love

Andrew Grey

INSIDE
ANDREW GREY
OUT

Dreamspinner Press

Published by
Dreamspinner Press
5032 Capital Circle SW
Suite 2, PMB# 279
Tallahassee, FL 32305-7886
USA
http://www.dreamspinnerpress.com/

This is a work of fiction. Names, characters, places, and incidents either are the product of author imagination or are used fictitiously, and any resemblance to actual persons, living or dead, business establishments, events, or locales is entirely coincidental.

Inside Out
© 2013 Andrew Grey.

Cover Art
© 2013 L.C. Chase.
http://www.lcchase.com
Cover Photo
© 2013 FLYFOTO.
http://flyfotoimages.com
Cover Model
Jesse Jackman.
Cover content is for illustrative purposes only and any person depicted on the cover is a model.

All rights reserved. This book is licensed to the original purchaser only. Duplication or distribution via any means is illegal and a violation of international copyright law, subject to criminal prosecution and upon conviction, fines, and/or imprisonment. Any eBook format cannot be legally loaned or given to others. No part of this book may be reproduced or transmitted in any form or by any means, electronic or mechanical, including photocopying, recording, or by any information storage and retrieval system, without the written permission of the Publisher, except where permitted by law. To request permission and all other inquiries, contact Dreamspinner Press, 5032 Capital Circle SW, Suite 2, PMB# 279, Tallahassee, FL 32305-7886, USA, or http://www.dreamspinnerpress.com/.

ISBN: 978-1-62798-262-7
Digital ISBN: 978-1-62798-261-0

Printed in the United States of America
First Edition
November 2013

ACKNOWLEDGMENTS

A special thank-you to Jesse Jackman for the use of the fantastic cover image. You were amazingly generous!

CHAPTER
ONE

THE ALARM sounded, and Bull grunted and reached over to the clock next to the bed, slapping it off. The damned thing kept buzzing, so he slapped it again. It still wouldn't shut up, so Bull actually looked at it and pressed the fucking "shut up" button. With the room now quiet, he rolled over and groaned softly. He remembered the huge bear of a man he'd brought home in the wee hours of the morning.

"Hey, bud, it's time to get up and get going," Bull said, lightly slapping the man's huge ass. Big or not, the guy had had no idea what to do with it, and last night's horizontal games had been fairly unmemorable. "I got things to do, and I'm sure you do too," Bull said a little louder before he pushed back the covers and got out of bed. The guy began to stir, and Bull walked into the bathroom, scratching his hairy belly as he went. He used the toilet and then took the opportunity to splash some water on his face before returning to the bedroom. His trick from the night before—he used the term loosely because the guy was too old to be truly classified as a trick—was just pulling on his pants.

"I left my card on the nightstand. Call me if you want to do this again." He smiled, but it only accentuated the wrinkles on his face. Bull couldn't for the life of him remember the guy's name, which was pathetic for both of them. His trick because he was so

1

unmemorable, and for himself because he'd had so many one-night stands he didn't bother to try to remember them any longer.

Bull smiled and nodded, stifling a yawn that the guy might take as an invitation to try to get them back to bed, and Bull had plenty of things to do. He grabbed a pair of sweats and stepped into them. He pulled on a T-shirt while the guy stepped into his shoes. "I'll see you out," Bull said and led the guy through his house toward the door. Bull lightly kissed the guy good-bye because, well, it seemed like the right thing to do. He watched the guy descend the stairs, then closed the door. After heading back to the bedroom, Bull stripped the bed and threw the sheets in the laundry hamper in the corner. He remade the bed and then walked into the bathroom, pulling off the T-shirt as he went.

He shaved his face and then his head. He loved the way his skin glistened in the light. It added to his image as a total badass, and that made his job that much easier. It also tended to keep most people away, which made his life a lot less fucking complicated. Leaving the remnants of shaving cream on his face and head, Bull shucked his sweats and started the shower. He waited for the water to warm, then stepped under it. Even though the sex from the night before hadn't been particularly satisfying, he didn't feel the need to take care of things himself, so he simply washed, rinsed, and then stepped out from under the water. He grabbed a towel and dried off before dropping it and standing in front of the mirror. "Fuck, I need to stop eating crap," he groused as he pinched his slight belly. He wasn't fat by any means, but he was big—another intimidation factor he loved. Bull added a stop at the gym to his day's activities. The fact was, he hadn't felt like doing anything all week and his chores were piling up, so he got dressed, pulled everything together, and got ready to leave.

He spent most of the day running his errands. He ended up at the gym in the early evening, which was fine, and did his workout. A few people he knew talked to him briefly at the gym, but other than that, he just did what he needed to do. After the workout, he cleaned up once again and then headed out to work at the club.

"Bull," Harry, his business partner, called as soon as he walked in the back door. "We're expecting a huge crowd tonight."

"I know," Bull answered flatly as he followed Harry back to the office area. He sat in his chair in the office. He thought about putting his feet on the desk, but Harry hated it, and he was one of the few people whose opinion mattered to Bull. In addition to being Bull's business partner, Harry was also the closest thing to a real friend that Bull had. "I've already told the boys to be on their toes, and I'll be out there the entire night." It was Bull's job to make sure the club remained secure and the crowd behaved. Sometimes it was a big job, like it was going to be tonight.

"These boys always bring in the crowd," Harry said with a smile that Bull allowed himself to share. Nights like this, with the dancers, always packed the place, and as long as he and his team could keep the patrons from sneaking in their own alcohol, they made a killing on the bar sales. "But sometimes…."

Bull shivered in the warm office. "I know. If I see that drug-dealing bastard, Carter, I'll throw him out myself, and this time I'll aim for the dumpster." That kind of shit always caused trouble, and on the nights when they brought in the exotic dancers, it was always worse. Harry knew how to run a club and how to bring in a crowd, and it was Bull's job to secure the club entrance and make sure the place was safe. They'd had a major fight a year earlier that had cost them thousands. There was no way they were letting that happen again. They had been unable to open for days because of repairs, and some items had to be brought up to current code because they were making repairs. Not to mention the danger to their license.

"It's not just Carter," Harry said.

Bull nodded slowly. He was well aware of that. "Let's get started, then." Harry stood, and Bull did as well. He left the office and headed out into the club, where he knew his team would be gathering. The bartenders were hard at work getting ready for the busy night. Glasses sparkled in the racks over the bar, and the tink of bottles hitting bottles reached Bull's ears as liquor was stocked. To Bull, it was the sound of money—lots of money.

3

"Okay, guys," Bull said as he approached the small group of four men who would be acting as bouncers this evening. "You all know the drill, but we've gotten wind of a new booze-smuggling scheme. They tape plastic bladders to their calves. So when you pat down, be sure to go all the way down to their ankles. Reggie, you did great last time finding those airline bottles. Keep it up and show the others." He nodded once in acknowledgement. "At the first sign of trouble, call. Do not wait until it escalates. This room is going to be filled with guys hyped up on testosterone from the show with their judgment impaired by alcohol." All four men nodded. "Any questions?" Bull asked and received headshakes. "Are there any questions?" he repeated more loudly.

"No," they all answered.

"Good. Use your voices to project power. It works. If you're quiet, they'll mess with you. The force of your voice can prevent you from having to use your hands." Bull looked at each of them. "Do you all have supplies of icy towels? If not, they're in the freezer in back and behind the bar." The bouncers nodded. "Where you can, use them instead of becoming physical." The simple application of a frozen towel to the back of the neck was a quick way to separate two patrons rather than putting the bouncer in harm's way. It also meant they didn't have to touch them, which was a plus. "Let's go to work. We open in ten minutes."

They all began to file away. "Keep your eyes open," Bull bellowed, and they all jumped. "See, the power of your voice. You all jumped. Make them do the same."

"Yes, sir," the four of them yelled, the sound echoing over the music that had just started blaring from the speakers. That earned them a smile.

They opened the doors on time, and Bull instantly felt his energy level rise and his senses sharpen as the first patrons walked through the door. At this hour they were few and far between, which was normal. People wouldn't really begin to arrive until ten. The show was scheduled to start at eleven. Bull checked all the stations around the club, touching base with the shirtless bartenders as well as the people posted at each of the doors.

An hour before showtime, Bull relieved one of the men at the door and stood at the front of the line. Everyone had to pay a cover, and on a night like this, no way would he let in any of the bouncers' friends, or the flirty twink who happened to catch their eye, for free. Every space in the club could be sold at least twice on a night like this, and it was his job, and to the advantage of his wallet, that he sell each of those spots.

By ten thirty, the line was long and becoming restless, because every twink, leather daddy, boy, slave, and dude in town wanted to see the members of the Philadelphia Inferno strip it all off, or as close to all as you could come in Harrisburg. A few fights broke out in line, and Bull either pulled men apart or used the towels to break them apart. He also sent those groups to the end of the line, which meant they were screwed for seeing the show. That ended the fight in a fucking hurry. No one wanted to land in nightclub purgatory, not after waiting an hour already. At ten minutes before eleven, a group of men approached the front of the line. They talked excitedly, and when their turn came, they stepped forward. There were three of them, all looking about twenty-one or twenty-two. He carded them. "I need to search you," Bull told the first one.

The kid stepped forward and lifted his arms. "Search away, hot stuff," he said, and as soon as Bull touched him, he began to giggle like a ten-year-old. Bull ignored it and checked the kid's belt and up his back, then down his chest. All the while the kid was giggling and squirming like a demented belly dancer.

"Please empty your pockets," Bull told him, and the kid turned out his pockets. Bull checked down his pant legs, and the kid began giggling again. "You got a problem?"

"You're tickling me," the kid said. Bull straightened up and crossed his arms over his chest.

"That's some act, kid. What are you hiding?" Bull asked. He'd seen more tries at distraction than he could remember, but this was definitely a new one.

"Nothing. I'm just ticklish," the kid said, the smile slipping from his adorably cute face and some of the light slipping from his eyes. What surprised Bull wasn't the way the kid stared back at him—something almost no one did—or the way his bottom lip stuck out just enough to make Bull want to smile. It was the disappointment he felt that the kid wasn't grinning anymore, because maybe he'd been smiling at him. Bull blinked that thought out of his mind. Pushing it away, he contemplated whether he should let the kid in.

"See how you react when someone's touching all your sensitive spots." Bull was about to tell the kid to take off when he reached out and ran his fingers over Bull's belly. "Aren't you ticklish?" he asked and continued working the tips of his long, slender fingers over Bull's T-shirt.

Bull had to work not to crack a smile. Not because it tickled in the least, but because this kid would be forward enough to actually touch him. "No," he snapped. "Move on inside before I change my mind."

The kid pulled back his hand and lifted big brown puppy eyes to him for a few seconds before heading into the club. Bull swore softly to himself as he watched the kid walk away. When he returned his attention to where it should have been the entire time, he saw Greg, the other bouncer working the door, staring at him with a stupid grin on his face. Bull growled at him, and Greg turned back to the line, continuing to let people inside.

At five minutes to eleven, Bull called a halt. "We're at our limit," he said loudly, and those waiting in line let out a collective groan. "You're welcome to wait, and we'll let people in as others leave, but there's nothing else we can do." The guys all groaned again, and a few of them stepped out of line, giving up quickly. Others pressed forward, and Bull growled. "Stay where you are or go home! Those are your choices. There's no more room, and that's by city regulation." The second guy in line stepped forward like he was about to argue, and Bull leaned down, getting right in the kid's face. "Don't even think about it."

The guy looked over his shoulder, swallowed hard, and stepped back into line. Bull said nothing, but continued staring at him, watching the fight leach out of him.

"I can take care of things here," Greg said.

Bull nodded. "You have any trouble, give me a call," Bull told him and then stepped inside the club.

The place was rocking. Music blared, and everywhere he looked, boys were dancing, drinking, and moving to the beat. Bull found the spot he liked so he could watch the crowd and waited until the music died and lighting shifted. Harry stepped out onstage in a sequined tuxedo, and the crowd quieted. He explained the rules in no uncertain terms and then proceeded to undermine his speech by working the crowd into an expectant, carnal frenzy. Then he introduced the first dancer.

Bull tore his gaze away from the dancer and scanned the crowd. He wasn't there to ogle or watch the strippers. He needed to stay focused on the crowd and potential trouble. The dancer began his routine, and Bull watched for people not watching the dancers. They were the ones there to cause trouble or with an agenda of their own. Everyone seemed to be watching the dancers, though. "Everything okay?" Harry asked, appearing next to him.

"Yes. They're having a good time. I'm going to check outside and make sure the line's okay. Then I'll be back." Bull moved around the edge of the undulating crowd toward the door. Everything was surprisingly quiet outside. The number of people in line had decreased considerably. There was nothing else he could do. Bull would love nothing more than to take their money, but it wasn't likely to happen tonight, at least not until the show was over. Bull nodded to Greg and then went back inside.

He turned toward the stage and saw the tickler jumping up and down near the stage. Bull watched him bounce and jump up and down as the police officer onstage tore off his shirt and whipped it around his head. The guy shone with oil—he had smooth, perfect pecs and a deeply grooved stomach above hips that rocked and swayed to the music.

7

Bull shifted his gaze back to where the ticklish guy was bouncing. Up and down, up and down... then, he didn't come up. Bull waited a few seconds and didn't see him. Instantly he began winding through the crowd, pushing guys to the side. One of the good things about being as big as he was: people usually moved out of his way. Bull reached the front of the crowd and pushed several guys to the side in time to see the kid curled in a ball on the floor. Bull bent down and lifted him into his arms. The guy didn't weigh much, and Bull began making his way back out. "Are you okay?" Bull asked as they approached the edge of the crowd.

"I think so," the kid said, and Bull held him closer before carrying him to the back of the club and off the main floor to a quiet area they used for medical issues or to give patrons a chance to cool off. Bull rested him on the sofa.

"Did you get trampled?"

"I guess. I lost my balance when the guy next to me shoved me out of the way, and the next thing I know, I was looking up at a forest of legs that I figured were going to pound on me at any minute." The kid took a deep breath. "I curled up to try to protect sensitive areas, and then you carried me out."

"Did you get kicked anywhere?" Bull asked.

"A little, but I think I'm going to be okay. Nothing really hurts." He stood up and took a few tentative steps. "Thank you."

"You're welcome. Be careful when you get back out there. The crowd is really wired," Bull warned. "Stay toward the back of the crowd. You should be able to see and still stay on your feet."

"I will," the kid said, and Bull led him out of the room and back to the club. Good as his word, the kid stayed toward the back, and Bull began scanning the crowd for trouble. However, he found he kept checking out the kid. As the dancing progressed, the energy and scent of testosterone in the room went through the roof. Bull kept an eagle eye on everyone and everything until the last dancer had wrapped up his routine. Only when the stage lights faded and the house music came on did he breathe a sigh of relief.

Reality quickly kicked in. Hundreds of men who'd been drinking and teased to within an inch of their libido-driven lives were not the recipe for calm. A fight began just behind him. Bull turned and grabbed one of the men while another bouncer toweled the other. He loved it when big men squealed like girls, and those frozen towels often made them do just that. Bull was in no mood to find out what had caused the fight. Instead, he and the other bouncer half carried both men to the door and out into the night. The doorman let in two men who'd been waiting, and Bull's night continued, with the routine repeating itself multiple times during the evening.

"So," Bull heard from behind him. He turned slowly to see Tickle Boy standing behind him. "Can I ask you something?"

"I'm working," Bull grunted and forced his gaze away from puppy-dog eyes, pouty lips, and a tight little body he wanted to do nasty things to. His pants tightened and Bull groaned. He so did not want to be doing his job with a hard-on for the rest of the night. Bull had learned long ago that his job did not involve getting turned on by anything he saw in the club. They had handsome dancers stripping to tiny G-strings at least twice a month, and he'd always been able to concentrate on what was important—his job. But this kid pulled his attention like nobody's business, and he needed to get his head in the game or something was going to happen and he'd miss it. His job was to keep order and try to keep his patrons safe, often from each other.

"I know. But I want to know if you're really as mean as you look."

Bull growled again and bared his teeth slightly. That had always been guaranteed to scare off even the stupidest drunk. But fuck if the kid didn't just stare at him. "I need to work."

"Okay, fine," the kid said and turned away. Bull watched him rejoin his friends, and they talked amongst themselves for a few seconds, glancing over at him. The kid coming to speak to him had probably been some kind of dare. Bull let his gaze roam over the crowd, but he saw nothing to catch his eye at the moment. Sure enough, within seconds he was staring at Tickle Boy.

"Someone has caught your eye," Harry said from next to him. He was now dressed in his normal, mostly black clothing.

"No. Just making sure the kid I helped earlier is all right," Bull said, turning his gaze to a group of men who were growing louder. He caught their attention and they instantly settled. He loved when he could stop an incident before it started.

"Sure you were," Harry said. Bull glared at him, growling under his breath, and Harry didn't push it. "So how have things been?"

"Not too bad, considering," Bull answered without pulling his attention from the club floor. The DJ was really rocking the crowd and the bar was three deep with men, but the boys were getting them through. "It's going to be a big night." Bull glanced at Harry, and he nodded slightly before moving off, most likely to check on other areas. Bull took a deep breath and let himself relax for just a few seconds. Things were going remarkably well.

Too well—within minutes, something reached his ears that didn't jibe with the music. He looked around and groaned loudly before taking off through the crowd. He approached the group of men just in time to see two guys pushing each other and others beginning to circle. "Break it up!" Bull projected over the music. They ignored him, and he called for help through his transmitter before jumping into the fray. One of the guys took a swipe at him. Bull dodged it, and damned if the other one didn't try the same shit. He wasn't so lucky the second time and took a punch to the cheek.

Bull growled and grabbed the guy, barrel-hugged him, and started toward the door. Yelling erupted behind him, and Bull twisted around, groaning under his breath.

"Let go of me," the guy he held cried, struggling and kicking Bull in the shin. Bull grunted and squeezed harder. Thankfully, one of the other bouncers arrived, and Bull shoved the guy in his arms at him and took off back to what was quickly escalating into a larger altercation. He and his men converged and began pulling people apart with brute strength, frozen towels, and every other tool they had. When Bull got to the bottom of the pile, he groaned. "I should have known," he said. He bent down to pull Tickle Boy to his feet, but then stopped. "Are you okay?"

The kid lifted his head slowly. His lip was bleeding, and he would definitely have one hell of a shiner. "I think so?"

"What did you do? Ask more people questions they don't want to answer?" Bull said, extending his hand. Tickle Boy took it, and Bull helped him to his feet. "Let's get you back where I can look at you." Bull led him to the same room they'd been in before. "Trouble seems to follow you, doesn't it?"

"It's not my fault," the kid said quickly.

"Somehow I find that hard to believe... or is it my company you can't get enough of?" Bull asked and instantly wondered why he'd asked that.

"Believe it or not, those two gorillas were fighting over me like I was some kind of damsel in distress." He touched his lip with his finger, and Bull handed him a tissue. "I'm Zach," the kid said.

"They call me Bull," he answered. He reached for another tissue and handed it to Zach. "You need to be more careful."

"I didn't do anything. Honest," Zach said, putting up his hand. "I was talking to this guy and the other one came up and started giving him shit about it." He lowered his gaze to his shoes. "Okay, I was probably flirting a little, but that's no reason for them to go all ape on each other. I didn't mean anything by it. I was just having fun. The guy with the tattoos was telling me what he wanted to do once we got back to his place." Zach shivered before squeezing his eyes closed and shaking his head. "Then the other guy, the one with the huge loops through his ears, started in. I was trying to get away, because I'm not some kind of boy slut, and the two of them started blaming each other, and then...." Zach stopped and dabbed his lip.

"Do you flirt with a lot of guys?" Bull asked. He took the tissues from Zach and threw them in the trash. He had an idea that Tickle Boy was as flirty as they came.

Zach shook his head violently. "Not usually. Today is my birthday, and the guys said I should let loose and have some fun. I didn't know it was going to get me punched," Zach said, and Bull

11

believed him. The kid seemed confused. "The whole seeing strippers thing was my birthday present." Zach smiled and then winced, touching another tissue to his lip. Then he stood up and walked toward the door. "Thank you for helping me. I didn't mean to cause you any trouble." Zach left the room, and Bull stood up as well. He threw away the last of the tissues and walked back to the club floor.

He scanned the dance floor, now pulsing with mostly shirtless guys dancing and having the time of their lives. "Looking for someone?" Greg asked with a knowing smile as he came up to Bull. "You haven't been able to take your eyes off that kid the entire evening." Bull didn't look at Greg. "See what he's doing after closing."

Bull continued looking for trouble, but found nothing other than guys having fun. "Make a run through the bathrooms and put the fear of God into anyone you find in there."

Greg held up his hands. "Sorry I mentioned anything." Bathroom duty was the worst and everyone knew it. Bull was instantly sorry he'd pulled rank on Greg. Nothing was ever going to happen between him and Zach. The kid was way too young, and Bull only did one-night stands. Zach might have been a flirt, but Bull knew once he delved into those brown eyes or found out just what Zach's pouty lips could do…. No, Bull never picked up guys at his own club. He went to other places, but never here. It was bad for business, and he certainly didn't want anyone knowing his personal business. As far as they were concerned, he had no life, and that was fine. No complications, no emotional attachments that led to dramatic scenes he didn't need.

For the rest of the night, Bull broke up a few fights and handled issues at the door, but other than that, he spent most of the evening watching people. More than once he saw Zach with his friends, laughing. He appeared to be having a good time. His eye had already darkened, but that was only getting the kid more attention. At one point, Harry called Bull back to the office. They talked briefly, and then he returned to the club floor. Much to his chagrin, he looked over the crowd, but didn't see Zach. More than once he cussed himself out under his breath for even looking, but the kid must have left. It was definitely for the best; Bull knew that. He wasn't looking for any complications, and that young man was a walking, talking complication if he ever saw one.

"Last call!" went up through the club. A number of the patrons groaned and then headed to the bar for a final drink. Half an hour later, the music silenced, and Bull and his team began the process of rounding up the stragglers and getting them on their way. That included calling cabs and making sure no one was too drunk to drive home.

At three in the morning, Bull locked the club and walked through the now silent and largely dark space. He both loved and hated the club like this. He loved it because it was quiet, and after an entire night of blaring music, he relished the silence. And he hated it because it was empty, but he tried not to dwell on that too much. Whenever he thought about it, Bull reminded himself of all the reasons why he avoided entanglements. "I don't need that shit," he muttered under his breath and hurried across the floor and into the office.

"Talking to yourself?" Harry teased as he worked at his desk. "Another success," he added when Bull dropped into his chair. "I'm almost done here." Harry yawned and shifted to open the safe. Harry counted the cash for deposit, and then Bull verified it before Harry placed the take in the safe.

With the safe door closed and locked, Bull gathered his things and got ready to leave. They had one hard and fast rule: after closing, no one left alone, so Bull walked Harry out, and they set the alarm and went to their cars. Bull said good night to his partner and drove to his apartment. Once he got inside, he locked the door and poured a scotch over ice and sat in his chair.

In the club, there was no one more depressing than the guy who drank alone. Bull took a sip of the liquor and then downed the rest in one swallow. He thought about having another, but set the glass on the table beside the chair and turned on the television for company. He was asleep in less than fifteen minutes.

ANDREW GREY

CHAPTER
TWO

ZACH SPENCER sat at his computer and yawned. His work was boring, but it paid his bills. He'd been lucky to get the job, something his boss seemed to relish reminding him of every chance he got. After finishing the design for stationery for one of his boss's clients, Zach stealthily opened his lower desk drawer and pulled out his notebook.

"What are you doing?" Kevin asked from the next cubicle. He always seemed to know when Zach had taken a few minutes from his work.

Zach sat up and looked down the hall toward his boss's office. Brantley Houseman was his boss, but he hadn't hired Zach directly. However, it was Brantley the Buttwad who Zach had been assigned to. Brantley was an account manager, and it was Zach's job to do whatever Brantley wanted. Since Zach had been trained as a graphic designer and artist, Brantley used him to create the visual designs he needed. "Just dreaming," Zach said and went back to his computer. He worked for a while, then he couldn't stand it any longer. He checked that Brantley was busy and pulled his sketchpad out of his drawer.

"Did you draw that?" Kevin asked from behind him, and Zach squeaked slightly.

"Don't do that, you'll scare me to death. I thought you were Brantley," Zach whispered. "Yeah, I drew them. Why?"

14

"They're really good," Kevin said. "I always knew Brantley was full of horseshit," he added, glancing toward the closed office door. "He likes to keep everyone under his thumb and he does it by lowering our self-esteem below his."

Zach showed Kevin some of his drawings and saw Kevin's eyes widen. "Isn't that the guy who helped you when we took you out for your birthday a few weeks ago? The bouncer." Kevin whistled softly. "You made him really hot. Not that the real guy wasn't attractive, but you drew him even hotter."

"That's the whole idea of comics. I get to take something in real life and make it better, hotter." Zach turned the page. "I call him Bull. He's the hero and he's in a constant battle with drug dealers and pimps to try to keep his portion of the city clean." Zach turned the page. "I haven't come up with his archenemy yet. That's taking a little more time than I thought it would. Somehow Bull has to cause one of the bad guys great pain. I've been thinking of having Bull throw drug dealer Hank out a window, and he'd get all cut up and come back as Attila the Hunk, intent on destroying Bull at all costs."

"Come on," Kevin said. "You gotta come up with better names than that. I like Attila, though. It's nasty-sounding and really conjures an image, but Hunk makes him sound too pretty. Attila the...."

Zach heard a door open and put away his notebook. "That should be what you need," Zach said a little louder than was necessary, and Kevin thanked him and got back to his desk. Zach managed to close his drawer in time.

"Are those designs done?" Brantley demanded.

Zach attached the files to an e-mail and pressed send. "They're in your inbox," he told Brantley with a smile and opened the next set of files to begin work. Zach had managed to come up with a number of interesting and clever designs for their clients, but he never heard much about them. Once he sent to them to Brantley, they always seemed to end up in a black hole, unless Brantley found something wrong. Then he'd get them back with snide comments so Zach

15

could fix them. "I'm working on the designs you wanted for Simpson Electronics now." Zach smiled, and Brantley grunted before turning around and heading back to his office.

"Make him your villain," Kevin whispered from his desk, and then he stuck his head around the cubicle wall. "He'd make a great villain."

Zach grinned and nodded. Kevin went back to his work. Zach, on the other hand, began running catchy phrases having to do with Brantley through his mind. They called him Brantley the Buttwad, but he wanted something better. Brantley the Asshole fit him perfectly, but it didn't fit the comic book character. Buttmunch Brantley came to mind, but it wasn't catchy enough. As a drug dealer, he could be known as Barbiturate Brantley, and after his transformation, Brantley the....

Brantley's voice carried through their work area, and Zach was thankful he wasn't looking for him. Still, he could feel everyone in the room cringe. Once Brantley's door closed, Zach peered over the wall. "Do you know Brantley's middle name?"

Kevin snickered. "Edgar," he said, and Zach giggled as he went back to his seat. "Edgar the Enema," Zach said, and Kevin snickered again. It worked. It was a play on "enemy," and there were all kind of interestingly depraved things he could do to Brantley that had to do with enemas: it was perfect.

Brantley bellowed again, and Zach pulled his mind out of his fantasies and got back to work. He didn't want Brantley yelling at him like that, and he certainly would if he found him daydreaming. Brantley the Slave Driver was an accurate description, but Zach kept that one to himself as he opened the files he needed and got back to work.

Zach worked for another few hours until, thankfully, it was time for lunch. He grabbed his sketchpad and his lunch bag and headed down to the lunchroom. The one good thing about Brantley was that he never ate in the lunchroom. He might have to talk to them, and that was something Buttwad didn't do unless he wanted something or was yelling at them, so at least lunch periods were safe from Brantley's bluster. Zach dropped his lunch at his usual table and went to the soda machine to get a Diet Coke before returning to his place. He opened his lunch and began to eat, and once he was done, he began to draw. For a few minutes, Zach entered a world of his own creation.

"Can I join you?" Kevin asked him, and Zach motioned toward the chair across from him. Kevin sat down and opened his lunch. "You should be careful about working on that here. If Brantley gets word of it, he'll use it against you somehow."

Zach sighed. He'd been getting an image of how he wanted Edgar to look, but Kevin was right. He should do that work at home. In fact, he reminded himself to take all his notebooks home to prevent Brantley from ever finding them. Zach closed the notebook in case someone was looking over his shoulder.

"Do you have plans tonight?" Kevin asked as he pulled a banana out of his bag and began peeling back the skin.

"No. I thought I'd stay home and work on the comic book. You're welcome to come over if you want, though. I need to stop at the store and get some stuff for dinner," Zach said, trying to remember if he had anything in the apartment to eat. He quickly concluded there was nothing he'd want to serve his friend.

"That would be cool," Kevin said. "My mother baked and sent some things with me the last time I visited. I could bring them along."

Zach nodded. "That would be great." He tried to remember the last time he'd had someone bake things for him. It turned out he couldn't ever remember that happening.

"Do you want to call some of the other guys?" Kevin asked. "We could sort of have a night if you want. It is Friday, after all."

"Sure," Zach said with a smile. He'd met Kevin when he'd started this job six months ago, and they'd almost instantly become friends. It started out because everyone in the office needed to join forces to survive Brantley, but quickly grew into a friendship Zach counted on. During his teenage years, Zach had quickly learned there wasn't much he could count on, so that said a great deal about

17

Kevin. "Why don't you follow me after work? Call the guys, and we can stop at the store and get everything we need for a pig-out. We can stop at your house along the way and get your stuff."

Kevin nodded and grinned. Then he pulled out his phone and began making calls.

Zach had lucked out when he had met Kevin. Making friends had never been particularly easy for him, but he'd always tried to make the best of his situation. There was little use in complaining or getting angry. All that did in the end was make things harder for him, so he smiled as best he could and carried on. Thankfully, it looked like things were going his way for once. He had a job, such as it was, and it paid his bills. He had friends and didn't, for the time being, need to worry about where his next meal would come from. So overall, life was pretty good.

"The guys will all meet at your place at seven," Kevin told him excitedly after hanging up the phone.

Zach checked his watch before gathering his things together. "Cool." He needed to clean up and get back to work or he'd be late. Zach rolled his eyes at the thought, but Brantley would come unglued, and it was Friday, so Zach wanted to end the week without getting yelled at.

"Yeah," Kevin said, echoing his unvoiced sentiment as he cleaned up his own lunch stuff. They got back to their desks just in time and spent the afternoon working. At the end of the day, they packed up and got out of the building before Brantley could decide he had some sort of emergency that required them to stay until it was sorted out. "Let's stop at my place first," Kevin suggested. "I can grab my stuff and ride with you."

"Do you want to stay on the couch tonight?" Zach asked, and Kevin seemed to think about that for a second before nodding. "Then let's go. I'll see you there." Zach walked to his car, a used one that was in really good shape. He wished he could have gotten something more fun, but his Camry was reliable and it provided the transportation he needed. He drove the few miles from his office in Lemoyne to Kevin's apartment in Camp Hill. He pulled in and parked next to Kevin's car. Within a few seconds, Kevin raced out of his building carrying his backpack and a plastic bag. Zach popped the trunk, and Kevin placed his stuff inside. He closed the lid and then pulled open the passenger door and slid into the seat. Then they were off to the store.

Zach pulled into the Weis Market and found a parking spot. He and Kevin hurried inside. The guys were going to be at Zach's in little over an hour, so Zach grabbed a cart at the door and they headed up the aisles. He did his regular shopping as well as getting what he wanted for the evening. "I need to get some things. I'll meet you at the checkout," Kevin said before taking off.

Zach made his way through the fresh vegetables and picked out what he needed. He'd be the first to admit he probably should have been watching where he was going, but as he moved forward, he looked up just before pushing his cart into someone.

"Watch where you're going," the guy said, whirling around.

Zach opened his mouth to apologize, but all that came out was, "Bull." He'd been seeing the guy from the club in his dreams for the past two weeks. Zach gaped at him, openmouthed, as he studied him. "Uh, sorry," Zach stammered as he pulled the cart backward. Bull's eyes narrowed like he was trying to place him. Zach smiled, because he couldn't help himself, and he saw the instant Bull remembered.

"Tickle Boy," he said, and Zach nodded, still grinning. At least Bull had remembered him.

"That's me," Zach said, touching his cheek, where the guy had punched him. It had hurt like heck at the time. "My eye was really ugly for a while." Bull was looking around, and Zach tried to think of something else to say. "I want to thank you for helping me that night. I'm not usually that flighty, and I'm sorry about the whole tickling thing." Now, that was a bald-faced lie. He wasn't sorry at all, because when he'd touched Bull's belly, he'd felt the ridges and the way Bull's muscles had moved under his touch. Zach had spent hours thinking of Bull and wondering what was under his shirt. He'd.... Zach felt himself blushing right there in front of the cucumbers as he thought about what he'd ended up doing most of the times he'd thought of Bull.

Bull nodded, his gaze still darting around, and Zach knew he was trying to get away, so Zach backed up and gave him room.

"I'll see you around, kid," Bull said.

"Zach," he said quickly, and Bull paused. "I'm Zach. I told you that night, and you're Bull, but you never told me what your real name is." Bull growled under his breath, and Zach remembered that sound from the night at the club. It went right to his groin and settled there. Zach closed his eyes for a second and thought unsexy thoughts, like Sunday dinner with his mother. Yeah, that would definitely kill any mood.

"Good-bye," Bull said and turned away.

"Are you working tonight?" Zach asked. He had no idea why he was pursuing this conversation or why he would do almost anything to keep Bull from turning away. The guy was menacing and could snap him in half like a twig if he wanted to. But then Zach remembered the way Bull had held him in his arms, carrying him after he'd been knocked over in the club that night, like he'd been precious. From the reception tonight, though, he figured he must have imagined everything he'd thought about for the past few weeks.

"Yeah. It's another big night. The same dancers you saw are coming in again," Bull said. "Look, I got to go or I'll be late for work." Bull turned and hurried away.

"Was that him?" Kevin asked as he approached. "That was. That was the real Bull. Did you tell him you're creating a character after him?"

Zach shook his head and watched Bull turn the corner at the end of the aisle. "Why would I? It isn't as if he's going to really care."

"Huh," Kevin grunted softly, and then Zach remembered what he needed to do and got a move on to finish the shopping. He made his way to the meat section to get some hamburger and saw Bull bent over the case, reaching to get something from the back. Kevin

20

nudged him, and Zach rolled his eyes without taking his gaze off the way Bull's super-tight jeans hugged his rear end. "That's not a big-guy butt, that's a strong-guy butt," Kevin said. Zach jabbed him with his elbow a little harder than he'd intended, and Kevin squeaked. Bull straightened and glared at the two of them before leaving. It took Kevin two seconds before he began snickering under his breath. Zach barely heard him. There had been something in Bull's expression that Zach didn't understand. It hadn't been anger or embarrassment, but something Zach couldn't quite read but thought he should understand. It confused him and left him standing in the aisle of the grocery store while others moved around him. "We should get going."

Zach nodded and absently wheeled his cart to the cereal aisle. He saw no sign of Bull, so Zach got what he needed before sending Kevin for milk while he hit the canned goods. As he turned the corner, Zach caught a glimpse of Bull walking away toward the far end of the store. He paused and watched him move. For a big guy, there was grace and fluidity in his movement, or maybe it was the way his backside swung back and forth like…. Bull looked toward him, and Zach's thoughts skipped like a needle on a record. The stormy-hurricane look from Bull made Zach turn away to examine the cans of green beans. This was stupid. Zach had allowed his imagination to run away with him again. Yes, Bull had been nice to him at the club, but that was his job. Regardless of how safe Zach had felt in Bull's arms or the way he'd tingled the few times Bull had touched him, it was all in his imagination.

Kevin put the milk in the cart, and Zach got the last of his canned goods, lingering a moment or two in the aisle before heading to the checkout. There was no sign of Bull, and Zach breezed through the checkout and out to the car. They loaded their purchases in the trunk, and then got in and drove to Zach's apartment.

They got there half an hour before the rest of the guys. Zach made some simple snacks and Kevin put out his mother's baked goods, then Zach got to work forming burgers. Their friend Jeremy was the first to arrive, followed by Tristan. They added their contributions to the evening's festivities and flopped in the living-room chairs. They chatted while Zach finished the last of the meal preparations before joining them. It was then he saw his sketchbook lying open on the coffee table.

"You should have told us," Jeremy said with admiration as he looked over the drawings. "These are amazing, and you have great detail here." Jeremy was the comic book guru of their group, and his opinion meant a lot to Zach. "You should have told us you were doing this." Jeremy never looked up from the book.

"I didn't really think they were that good. It's just something I do to relax," Zach said, feeling exposed and vulnerable. "It's sort of my thing for me."

Jeremy turned the page and looked up, his eyes wide. Then he glanced at the others. "That's the bouncer," he said. "Damn, you made him even hotter than real life."

"We saw him at the store a little while ago. He and Zach were talking," Kevin said. *The bigmouth.*

"I ran into him with my cart," Zach explained. "By accident," he added with a dramatic roll of his eyes.

"Sure you did," Tristan teased, and the others got in on the act. Zach shook his head and closed the sketchbook to put it away.

"Bring that back," Jeremy said. "I wasn't done." Reluctantly, Zach handed the sketchbook to Jeremy, who went through the entire book without saying anything or looking up from it. "This is amazing," he finally said once he'd looked at every panel. "You've got to do something with this. Finish your story, and I'll e-mail some friends about it." The others stared at Jeremy. "What? I've been going to comic book conventions since I was eight. I know everybody or know people who know everybody. Finish the story, and we might be able to get some people to look at it."

"Really?" Zach asked, but he kept a slight distance from the others. The three of them had been friends for a long time, and Zach still felt like a bit of an outsider. Not that they had necessarily done anything to tell him that; it was just how he felt, how he always seemed to feel about everyone in his life—he was there, but the perpetual outsider.

22

Jeremy stared at him openmouthed and then jumped to his feet and engulfed Zach in a hug. "Yes, really. You're one of us, in case you didn't know it. God," he added dramatically, squeezing him again and then letting go. "So do you have the whole story yet for the comic?"

"No. It's coming, though. I think I have my villain," Zach said and pulled another sketchbook from his bookshelves made of bricks and painted boards. Most of his furniture was things he'd managed to cobble together. It was what he could afford, so he lived with it. At least everything was clean and belonged to him. Zach sat down and began sketching. "I decided to do something based on Brantley." He glanced at Kevin. "We were throwing out ideas earlier, and we bounced around Edgar the Enema, but I'm not sure."

"The name isn't as important as the villain's behavior and theme. Once you have that, the rest will come," Jeremy said. "Just make sure you have a good visual and that the villain behaves consistently and has a good reason to hate the hero."

Zach nodded. He knew all that. He just needed to come up with an idea that would be different. "I need to think about it."

"Maybe you could put your character on a ranch or something, with a name like Bull," Tristan offered, but Zach and the others weren't convinced.

"If you're going to use an actual Bull persona, then he needs to have some connection to the real thing," Kevin said.

Jeremy shifted and looked over Zach's shoulder as he continued drawing. Zach had learned at some point that sometimes his ideas just came out through his hands rather than through words, so he quietly continued working. "You know, I think you should let Bull be Bull," Jeremy said softly. Zach stopped and turned to look at him. "It's obvious the guy at the club captured your attention, so use that. Make Bull a bouncer at the club, and a villain who fits into that world." Jeremy grinned, and Zach wondered what he was up to. "I think tomorrow night we should help Zach here with some research."

23

"No way," Zach said. "The guy isn't interested in me. At the store I talked to him for two seconds, and he couldn't get away from me fast enough. How am I supposed to get him to talk to me so I can ask him about what he does?"

"That's the beauty of my idea. You don't have to ask him anything. We can go to the club, dance, and have a good time while we watch what Bull does, and how he reacts." Jeremy leaned closer. "We could arrange for a little trouble to break out so you'd get to spend a little more time in Bull's back room." Jeremy was most definitely a horndog.

"All he did was help me and then walk me back out to the club," Zach explained and then looked at his shoes.

"But that's not what you wanted, was it?" Tristan teased, and Zach slapped his arm lightly. They all knew that Zach had never been with anyone, but then, neither had Kevin or Tristan. The experienced one in their group was Jeremy.

"Knock it off, Tristan," Kevin said lightly.

"So, are you guys in for a little research trip tomorrow?" Jeremy pressed, and the others all agreed. Zach went along because as long as he was with his friends he felt safe, and yeah, if he planned to base a character on Bull, he needed to have some material, and he didn't want to make up something lame. He could always take a tidbit from reality and make it more fantastic. "Good," Jeremy said. With that settled, they all turned their attention to food and worked together to finish up dinner. Jeremy had brought mac and cheese, and he heated it in the microwave while Zach cooked the burgers. The others pulled out what they brought, and once everything was ready, they set the feast out on the coffee table.

"So our little Zach has the hots for the bouncer," Tristan said once everyone had a plate and had begun to eat.

"Tristan," Kevin said warningly.

"Hey, I think it's cool," Tristan added.

Zach leaned forward slightly. "I don't have those feelings for you, Tristan, I'm sorry. We're just friends." Zach patted him reassuringly on the shoulder. Everyone went silent, including

Tristan, and then they all burst out laughing. It was painfully obvious to all of them that they *were* friends, nothing more.

"God," Tristan said when the laughter died down. "I was just beginning to wonder if anyone would catch our Zach's eye. At least now we know he likes them tall, huge, and scary." Tristan wriggled his fingers, and everyone laughed again.

"He's not that scary," Zach said. "Yeah, I know he looks intimidating and all, but I don't find him scary. He was nice to me, and there was this look in his eyes when he was helping me after I'd been hit." Zach looked at the other guys and saw only disbelief. "Okay, yeah, maybe I'm seeing what I want to see, but I swear it was there."

"I think you were probably seeing what you wanted to," Tristan said. "But who am I to judge? I sort of dated that guy two months ago, remember?" They all nodded. "Raoul—he was a real loser." Of course they remembered that. None of them could forget. He'd been so excited about it. He'd even gone out to get new clothes so he'd look just right. Tristan had called less than an hour after his date was scheduled to start and told them he was back at home. "I never told you guys...."

"Did he just want to jump in the sack?" Jeremy asked, and Tristan shook his head.

"He wanted a date to the gay version of a nerd party. I should have known when a guy like that asked me out. Yeah, you might be seeing what you want, so be careful, but you could also be seeing something everyone else is missing." Tristan looked at all of them. "Sometimes the outside is very different from the inside. Raoul was pretty and really nice on the outside, but he turned out to be a real dick. And not the good kind." It was obvious Tristan was still smarting from the way Raoul had treated him.

"You know you didn't deserve to be treated that way," Zach said. "Raoul was a real ass." He looked at the others, who nodded. "But it had nothing to do with you." Zach set down his plate and walked around the coffee table. He gave Tristan a hug. "People can be cruel beyond belief, sometimes with very little effort. But that

25

doesn't mean you did anything to bring it on," Zach whispered only to Tristan and then released him before returning to his place.

He took a bite of his mac and cheese and saw the others staring at him. "How—" Tristan began.

"You never talk about yourself," Jeremy interrupted.

Zach shrugged. "There's nothing really to talk about." He knew that wasn't exactly true, but he didn't like talking about his past. It wasn't particularly happy, and people didn't like to hear everyone else's sob stories. At least that was what he believed. "I grew up, graduated from college, and got the job working with Kevin." He looked around the sparsely furnished room and tried to think of some way to change the subject. "So, what time do you want to meet tomorrow to go to the club?"

The others exchanged looks. "We don't need to get there too early. There won't be anything happening before ten," Jeremy said.

At least they'd let the subject of his past go, and Zach breathed a small sigh.

"But if we go early, Zach might have a chance to talk to Bull before he gets too busy." Jeremy nudged him playfully.

"Okay," Tristan said. "I brought some movies we can watch if you want." Zach wanted to hug Tristan again for shifting the focus of the conversation. "I got *Beautiful Thing*—gay boys in England; it's really touching. I've also got *Latter Days,* and I brought *Kinky Boots.*"

"Isn't that a play or something?" Jeremy asked.

"It was a movie first," Tristan said and began digging through his bag. "It's about a failing shoe company and the owner decides to make boots for drag queens in order to try to keep from going out of business. It's a real hoot." He came up with the DVD and handed it to Zach, who opened the case and slid it into the player. The other guys had Blu-ray, but the player he had was older, so he made do. They all turned their attention to the television and the movie. After about an hour, they took a break and cleaned up the dishes. Zach put away what was left of the food, and everyone took a turn in the

26

bathroom. Then they piled on the sofa and watched the rest of the movie.

Once the shoe factory had been saved, they put in *Latter Days.* By the time the movie was ending, Zach was fighting to stay awake. When the DVD was over, Tristan and Jeremy got ready to leave. They agreed to meet at Jeremy's the following night, and after shared hugs, they left. Zach got his extra set of sheets and made up the sofa for Kevin. "Are you going to be comfortable out here?"

"Of course," Kevin told him with a slight smile. "I just need to clean up and stuff and I'll be all set." He grabbed his bag and headed to the bathroom. "Good night."

Zach said good night as well and went to his small bedroom. It barely qualified as a bedroom, with its small closet and just enough room for a twin-size bed, but it was all his, so he didn't care how big it was. Zach began getting ready for bed, and once he heard Kevin finish in the bathroom, he took his turn. After returning to his bedroom, he closed the door and stripped to his underwear before slipping between the sheets. He listened to see if Kevin needed anything, but the apartment was quiet. He stared up at the ceiling and smiled. His life was pretty good. Sure, his boss was a jerk, but he could live with that for now.

He rolled onto his side and closed his eyes, yawning once as he tried to settle down. His mind made a quick trip through his day and then settled on what he was afraid was becoming an obsession—Bull. He'd tried to push his fascination with the man away, but it kept coming out in his drawings, and now that he'd seen him again, he couldn't push him out of his mind. Rather than trying, Zach rolled onto his back and pushed down the covers. He closed his eyes and conjured up Bull standing in his room, staring down at him. Zach ran his hand down his chest as the imaginary Bull pulled off his shirt. He liked hairy men, so he gave Bull a thickly haired chest. God, he wanted to know what Bull's skin would feel like against his. Zach slipped his hand inside his shorts and cupped himself before pushing the fabric out of the way. He stroked himself as Bull came closer, took him in his arms, and kissed him. Zach imagined that Bull would be forceful, sliding his hands down his back before cupping his butt. He touched himself, pressed his finger to his opening and pretended Bull was touching him, tapping his opening while their cocks slid beside each other.

Zach spit on his hand and stroked faster, slipping a finger just inside. He imagined Bull's thick fingers stretching him. He stroked faster, hoping he wasn't making noise as the scene in his mind became more intense. Bull lifted him off his feet and gently laid him on the bed. He kissed him and slowly pressed inside, stretching and filling him. Zach continued stroking himself as Bull began to move. Harder and faster, Bull snapped his hips and drove deep inside him. Zach arched his back and moaned softly as his passion increased.

Zach pressed two fingers deep inside, imagining they were Bull's thick cock. He had a fertile imagination and let it take him on a passionate trip he knew he'd never be able to take in real life. Zach stroked his cock, pausing a few times to add a little moisture before continuing. When his fantasy Bull pushed his hand away and began stroking his cock while he fucked him, Zach whined and knew he wouldn't last much longer. He squeezed his cock tight and stroked a few more times before clamping his eyes tighter. Pressure built in his balls, and he tried to hold it off as long as he could before coming in an openmouthed rush.

He lay there, floating for a while, breathing as evenly and quietly as he could. Once his mind began to work again, he listened, hoping like hell he hadn't made enough noise for Kevin to hear. When he heard nothing at all from outside the room, he quietly opened the drawer next to the bed and grabbed a couple tissues. He cleaned up and discarded his mess before pulling up his underwear and rolling onto his side. Within a few minutes, he felt chilled, so he yanked up the covers and closed his eyes. He was asleep within seconds, still smiling. The only thing that could make him happier would be to have the real Bull with him. Like that was ever going to happen.

CHAPTER
THREE

"WHAT'S BEEN eating you?" Harry asked, standing next to Bull as the evening was just getting started. "It's a Saturday night and we're raking it in hand over fist." Harry practically vibrated with excitement.

"I don't know," Bull said as he rubbed the top of his smooth head. "Everything seems fucked up, and I don't have a clue why."

"Do you need to get laid?" Harry asked, and Bull rolled his eyes. "I'll take that as a no. So it's more than that?" Harry signaled the bartender, who brought over a glass and placed it right near Harry before going back to work. "Want one?"

"What is it? Whiskey?" Bull asked, judging from the color.

"Iced tea," Harry said, and then he sipped from the glass. "Let everyone think I'm having a drink. Hell, let them think you're having one. I only take a belt after the club closes, you know that."

"Thought maybe you were trying something new," Bull said.

"Nope, but it sounds to me you might consider it," Harry said. Bull huffed, and Harry set his glass on the bar. "Knock that off. It's me you're talking to, not one of these punk kids. You can growl all you like, but I don't give a shit; I've known you too damn long." Harry stared at him. "I think I know you better than you know yourself sometimes. This business is hard. It takes long hours and you have to be a bear to people sometimes to keep them from

29

ripping you off. But that doesn't mean we don't deserve someone to go home to." Harry put up his hand. "And I don't mean some twink or bear you pick up at some other place 'cause you won't cruise here."

"Jesus, can't I have some secrets?" Bull groused.

"Not from me. Those guys don't mean anything and you know it. So maybe what you need is to find someone who does mean something."

Bull chuckled deeply, folding his arms over his chest. "Look who's talking."

Harry chuckled in return. "You may think you see everything, but sometimes the most obvious thing is what's going on right under your nose." Harry picked up his glass and walked back to his office. Bull watched him, wondering what in hell Harry was talking about. They worked almost the same hours, and he'd never seen Harry interested in anyone, at least not here at the club.

Bull pushed away from the wall where he'd been leaning and decided to check on the door. He stepped outside and looked down the line. He groaned softly when he saw a certain pair of brown eyes peek out of line and meet his gaze. His first instinct was to look away, but this wasn't grade school, and he was in charge here.

He helped the guys at the door check people, and when Zach and his group approached, he saw Zach's friends all confer. Zach shook his head at first, but the others were obviously putting him up to something. Zach stepped away from the group, looking back at his friends, who all nodded. Then Zach walked right up to him and put his arms in the air. "You can search me if you like," he told Bull, his shirt riding up to show a strip of tanned belly skin.

Bull was tempted to call over one of the other guys, but he patted Zach down, who giggled like before. "Do you always do that?" Bull asked as roughly as he could. He was about two seconds from laughing himself, though he wasn't going to allow that. "Did your friends put you up to this?" he whispered as he finished his pat-down.

"Kind of," Zach told him as he stopped wriggling. "You're tickling me."

Bull rolled his eyes. This kid was delicious, with his tight little body, his butt poured into jeans that had to be a full size too tight. Bull stood back up and realized Zach wasn't that little, just in comparison to him. "You can go on inside," Bull said levelly. He expected Zach to move on, but he stood there. "Is there something you wanted?"

"Would I be able to talk to you for a few minutes later?" Zach asked.

"Do you want a job as a bouncer?" Bull asked with a grin. That was the usual reason people wanted to speak to him. Zach looked down at himself and then back up. Bull could almost see him wondering if he was serious. "I was joking. If you want to talk to me, move on inside, and when I have a few minutes, I'll find you."

Zach nodded and moved into the club.

Bull motioned to the next guy in line, patted him down, and of course found the airline bottle he'd clumsily tried to hide under his belt buckle. He took the bottle and threw it hard into the trash barrel, listening for the satisfying crash of breaking glass while he contemplated kicking the guy out of line to set an example. "You can go on in, but if you ever try anything like that again, I'll bar you from the club," Bull said loudly enough for the people in line to hear. "The next guy I find alcohol on isn't getting in," Bull boomed over the line. "And if I find drugs on you, we're simply calling the police."

Bull signaled the next guy and noticed that a number of the men left the line. He didn't know why and he didn't care. He did find a few containers on a few intrepid partiers, and true to his word, he sent them packing.

Once the line was under control, Bull left Greg in charge and went back inside. The beat of the music thrummed through the building, and every patron seemed to add to it. The excitement was electrifying, and it both thrilled Bull and raised his radar for trouble. On nights like this, when everything and everyone was all energy, spirits tended to run high. He scanned the room and saw Zach sitting with his friends at one of the tables. He watched them talk, and then Zach looked over at him and smiled. One of the guys Zach was with stood up, and Zach took his place. It looked like they'd switched places so Zach could watch him.

Bull immediately wondered what was going on with these guys.

"Something wrong?" Bob, one of the bartenders, asked, leaning over the bar.

"I don't know," Bull said, glancing away from the table for a few seconds.

Bob nodded and moved on to the next customers. Bull scanned the room and didn't see any trouble. He did catch Bob's eye and gave him a nod and a quick smile of thanks before heading toward the table. He figured he'd see what Zach and his group were up to.

"Having a good time?" he asked the group with a smile. They all looked up, all smiles and not a hint of guile from any of them. He turned to Zach. "You wanted to talk to me?" Zach nodded and stood up. Bull led him toward the back and to one of the vantage points Bull liked best. Troublemakers tended to watch the bar or the door, some the restrooms, depending on what they had in mind, but few paid any attention to the spot just behind one of the sets of lights. "What do you need?" The music wasn't as loud in this particular spot. That was another advantage. "You aren't looking for a job, are you?"

"No, but I wanted to ask you about your job," Zach said, shifting a little nervously from foot to foot. "I like to draw, and I'm starting this comic book, well, really, it's a graphic novel, and...um … I based my hero on you."

"Me?" Bull asked skeptically. "The hero," he added and then laughed. "I can see being cast as the villain, but definitely not the hero." Bull swallowed when Zach stared at him seriously. "I thought you were kidding."

"The last time I was here, you saved me. What's not heroic about that?" Zach asked and pulled a small notepad out of his pocket. Bull wasn't convinced, but if the kid wanted to use him as some sort of hero, he wasn't going to complain. "I was hoping you could maybe tell me some interesting stories about things you've seen, fights you've broken up, stuff like that. I'm trying to work on the plot of the story. I have great characters and an interesting villain, though that may change."

Bull shook his head. "Let me get this straight: you're creating a comic book, and I'm the hero?"

"A character based on you, yeah," Zach told him. "I wasn't sure if you'd be interested, but we all agreed"—Zach looked over at the table where his friends sat—"that you should know. It's only fair." Zach shifted again. "So will you help me?"

Activity on the other side of the club caught Bull's attention. Without answering, he hurried away toward raised voices and two men already squaring off with each other. "There a problem, guys?" Bull asked as he approached the two men. They weren't very big, and both of them took one look at Bull and swallowed as he loomed over them. "Either work it out or leave. But if you fight in here, I'll throw you out, and your mamas can come pick up the pieces." Both men shook their heads and backed away, heading to their respective groups. He watched for a few minutes and then walked back.

"What was that about?" Zach asked.

Bull shrugged. "I'm not their therapist. It's my job to make sure they don't cause trouble here or directly outside the club. We need to keep our lines controlled, and we try to be good neighbors to the businesses and the people who live in this area. I don't want people fighting in or outside my club, just like I don't want people dealing or doing drugs. It's bad for business." Bull tensed when he saw another potential situation developing. It seemed to settle on its own, though, and he relaxed.

"I need to let you work," Zach said. "I really appreciate you talking to me, though, and I'd like to hear some of your stories. I think it could add a touch of realism to the comic." Zach looked about ready to turn to go back to his friends. Bull knew he should let him, but dang, the kid was using him as his comic book hero.

"I don't get done until really late tonight, but I'm off tomorrow. We could meet somewhere if you want to talk," Bull offered.

From the smile he got, Bull would have thought Zach had just won the lottery. "Really?"

"Sure. How about we meet at the diner on Second near the Hilton, about one," he offered. He could give Zach some time. He had to eat anyway.

"Okay. I'll bring my drawings so you can see them," Zach said and then bounded back toward his friends. Damn, it looked like his feet barely touched the ground the whole way. Bull chuckled to himself for a few seconds and then stilled. How long had it been since he'd laughed about anything? He tried to remember and came up short.

"Is everything okay?" Harry asked as he approached him from behind. Bull didn't jump, but he had to consciously keep his hands to his side.

"One of these days, I'm going to knock your lights out when you do that," Bull said.

"Yeah, yeah," Harry said. "So who's the guy you were talking with?"

"He's just a kid," Bull said.

"No, he's a young man," Harry said, and Bull stifled a cringe when Zach looked back at him and smiled. This was not going to go well. "Really nice-looking, and he seems to like you."

"Harry," Bull warned.

"Knock it off. I have no idea what happened to you, but you've gotten growlier by the day. So you either need to get laid or fall in love."

"Harry the romantic," Bull retorted.

"I'm right, aren't I?" Harry quipped with a grin. "And since you never had trouble with the former, I'd say it's problems with the latter that are giving you fits." Harry turned toward him. "You can try to deny it, but that kid's getting to you."

"He is not," Bull countered lamely. "I just need a day off."

Harry gave him one of his "I know you better than that" looks. "Have you figured it out yet?" Harry asked.

Bull groaned. "It's not my job to babysit you or your love life. If you're seeing someone and they make you happy, that's all that counts. But you don't need to keep it a secret. No one around here is going to judge you."

Harry glanced toward the bar. A few minutes later, a glass of iced tea made its way over to him.

"Good for you," Bull said. How he could have missed it was beyond him. But like Harry said, it wasn't his job to watch his partner. "So which one is it?"

"Juan," Harry said. "We aren't keeping it a secret, except it's new and neither of us wants complications at work. He has to work with the other bartenders, and we need to manage the entire staff without playing favorites."

Bull knew that was true. He caught the eye of one of the other bouncers and saw him turn away for a second. He waited and watched as he moved toward the door. Bull followed his gaze and saw the problem. He was ready to help, but it wasn't needed. His gaze automatically went back to Zach and his friends. Harry chuckled softly, and Bull suppressed a growl. They weren't doing any fucking good anyhow. "Don't say a word."

"Wouldn't dare," Harry said and moved away. Bull saw his shoulders bouncing and knew the asshole was laughing.

Bull spent the rest of the night watching the crowd and doing his job. More than once he chastised himself for watching Zach when his mind wasn't occupied. His job was to watch the patrons and protect the club, but Zach drew his attention like a moth to flame. That scared the living crap out of him, not that he was about to tell anyone. He had his reputation to uphold. The patrons behaved because half of them were scared to death of him, and the other half had heard the stories. The other employees and bouncers respected him and were probably a little scared too, but that kept them on their toes, because if they messed up, they had to deal with him. If they knew a kid like Zach could get under his skin with a few giggles and puppy-dog eyes, he'd never be able to do his job.

After midnight, Zach and his friends got up to leave. Bull turned away and tried to look interested in what was happening over by the bar. "Thank you," Zach said, and Bull turned. "I'll see you at lunch. It's really cool of you to do this." Zach smiled and then turned back toward his friends. Bull watched him go and wondered what in the hell a cute little spitfire like Zach could ever see in a big lummox like him. The answer, of course, was nothing. He'd meet Zach for lunch, help him with his project, and then probably never see him again. And that was for the best. Right now, he had work to do, and Bull got back to it.

Keeping his mind on his tasks worked for most of the night, but as it wore on, he got tired and his mind definitely began to wander. By closing time, he was exhausted. Some of the other club staff members were organizing an after-hours party, but he begged off and went right home. Harry said he and Juan would handle closing the club, and Bull figured he didn't need to be a third wheel. At home, Bull took his customary single shot of scotch and went right to bed.

THE ALARM went off at noon, and Bull wanted to throw the damned thing across the room and then sleep for hours. He had the day off, which meant the night off, and he wanted to make the most of it. He didn't have to be anywhere…. "Shit," he said as he remembered his promise to Zach. There *had* been a reason he'd set the alarm. He got out of bed and shuffled to the bathroom. He used the toilet, shaved, and brushed his teeth before hopping into the shower.

An undercurrent of excitement ran through him as he washed. He was going to see Zach. He couldn't help wondering what the trim man would look like naked. He'd gotten a glimpse of belly when Zach had raised his hands over his head. Without thinking, Bull took his cock in his hand and slowly began to stroke himself.

36

He was just getting into it when a ringing interrupted his fantasy. Bull knew he should have turned his damned phone off. The ringing stopped, but the mood was gone, so he finished up and stepped out. He dried himself and wrapped the towel around his waist before leaving the room.

He picked up his phone off the dresser and checked the last number—his mother—and he groaned before putting it right back. "What in hell does she want?" he asked out loud to the empty room. He decided to ignore the call and the inevitable message. He got dressed and grabbed his wallet and keys. Reluctantly, he picked up his phone. By some miracle, there was no message, but she'd call him back. She always called him back.

Bull left the apartment. It was gorgeous outside. The sun was shining and birds were chirping in the trees. There were times when he almost felt vampiric, given the amount of time he spent awake after dark. After jogging slowly down the stairs, he got in his car and started the engine. Checking the time, he saw he could just make it to the diner without being late. He pulled out of his parking space and headed downtown.

By some luck, he found a place to park and walked into the diner just a few minutes before the hour. Zach was already seated at one of the tables, chewing his lower lip. Bull walked over to the table and slid into the seat across from him.

"You actually came," Zach said and grinned. "I brought my sketches so you could see them."

"Of course I came. I said I would," Bull said more harshly than he meant to. People in his life tended to say one thing, but do another. Bull hated that and always found a way to meet his commitments. Of course, the easiest way for him was to not make any commitments, but he had, so he was here regardless of whether this was a good idea or not.

"You didn't have to come," Zach said, packing up his things.

"I didn't mean to snap. I just got up and haven't had my coffee yet," Bull explained. Zach stopped what he was doing, looking at Bull skeptically.

"You're not at work, so you can drop the tough-guy act," Zach said.

"It's not an act," Bull said.

Zach smiled and shook his head. "No one can be that full of himself." Zach opened his sketchpad again and flipped through the pages before turning it around so Bull could see it. He stared at the drawing and felt his mouth fall open. "I could make you an asshole and turn the character into a villain, but I don't see him that way."

"I think I'm glad," Bull said, and then he actually smiled.

"See? I knew you weren't an asshole all the time," Zach said with a huge grin that Bull wanted to either smack or kiss off his face.

Bull blinked a few times. He had to keep thoughts like that out of his mind, because it wasn't going to happen. The server approached their table, and Zach reached for a menu. "I'll have the usual," Bull told her, and Zach ordered a hamburger and fries. The server put her pad in her apron and walked away, then returned with glasses of water and a mug of coffee for Bull. "That's what you see when you see me?" Bull asked once the server had left.

"Yeah, I guess," Zach said. "I mean, I make things up so they're more comic-bookish, but yeah. I used you because this is how you make me feel. I could have been stomped to death, but you got me out." Zach flipped the page. "I know it sounds kind of dumb, but you were nice."

"Aren't people nice to you all the time?" Bull asked and then sipped from his mug. The coffee was strong, but tasted dang good.

Zach humphed. "So would you tell me some stories about things that have happened at the club? I know you've probably encountered all kinds of stuff, and I'm trying to find a plot to go around my character." Zach set down his sketchpad. "I was thinking of calling him Bull, if that's all right, and I thought about giving him horns, like a bull. Maybe he could gore or charge the bad guys." Zach smiled again, and Bull would have spilled national secrets if he'd had any. This guy was so innocent and open; it had been a long time since he'd met someone like that.

38

"I don't think I can help you much there," Bull said. "I haven't picked up a comic book in a long time." He alternated his gaze from the drawing to Zach. The character Zach had created based on him was cool, with muscles and intensity. Basically, the drawing was hot. Bull had never seen himself that way. He'd always emphasized the intimidating and forceful; the rest he wasn't concerned about. Intimidating was safe and kept people at a distance. That was what he wanted, or at least what he thought he wanted.

"It's okay," Zach said. "I'm sure it will come to me." Then he smiled, and damned if Bull didn't smile back. "I was hoping you could tell me stories about what it's like to be a bouncer. I'm going to make this a gay comic and I want it set around a club. But I need action and drama. I've been thinking of having Bull go after a group of drug dealers or something, but that seems predictable."

"It depends on the club," Bull told him. "We're very strict. Harry—he's my business partner—and I decided when we opened the club that we didn't want to be that kind of place. If we find drugs on someone, we don't let them in. If we see them doing drugs in the club, we kick them out. Always have. So the people who want to do that stuff usually go someplace else." Bull smiled. "A few months ago I had this cool dude who parked right outside the club. He got out of his Porsche and walked right up to the door." Bull chuckled softly. "He came up to one of my men and offered him a deal to get into the club. My guy signaled one of the other bouncers and let him in the club."

"You did?" Zach asked.

"Sure. We called the police, and he had enough stash on him that he isn't going to see the light of day again for years. He was also seen actively dealing, so the 'cool dude' is sitting his ass in prison and his car was towed away by the police and impounded. He's done, and very few of his kind try to get in. Word gets around, both good and bad."

Zach pulled out a notepad and began writing. "That's really good. Edgar the Enema can be a drug kingpin who desperately wants to take over Bull's club because Bull helped put him in

39

prison, and that's where he was introduced to all kinds of kinky butt play."

Bull couldn't help laughing. "Edgar the Enema?" Bull asked.

"Yeah," Zach said, his smile dimming slightly. "My boss at work is a real douche. His middle name is Edgar, so we had to come up with something catchy. I may change it, but that's the working name."

"No, I like it. You can do some interesting things with that. Maybe he's developing a new super drug or something and it's most potent when taken as an enema. You could have a scene with him testing it and guys are bent over with their butts in the air or something, begging for it like they would sex, but it's the drug. It's a comic book, so you want fantastic, but sexy too, I would think."

Zach continued writing as the server returned with their plates. "Is there anything else I can get you?" she asked with a smile.

"I think we're good," Bull said before adding, "except maybe some more coffee."

"Sure, hon, I'll be right back." She walked away, then returned with the pot and filled his mug. He thanked her and turned his attention to the food. His stomach growled loudly, and Zach stopped eating and began to laugh.

"I have more questions, but they can wait until after you eat," Zach said.

"My stomach growls like the rest of me," Bull said before taking a large bite of his eggs. "What do you do besides draw comics and work for a douche?" he asked and then took a sip of his coffee. He was finally beginning to feel awake and with it.

"I work at a graphic design firm developing designs and logos for business cards, corporate letterheads, stuff like that. At least, that's my job description. What I really do is whatever Brantley wants. He's my manager. He didn't hire me, though, and I think he's got his nose bent out of shape over that." Zach ate a french fry. "But it's a job, and I can support myself and don't have to rely on other people." Zach picked up his burger and took a small bite.

Bull caught Zach's reference and narrowed his eyes, wondering why the happy, smiling man across the table from him would worry about having to rely on other people. He could see Zach smiling and crooking his finger at people and having them jump to do his bidding. "I understand not wanting to depend on others," Bull commented and then took another bite to stop himself from talking.

Zach looked down at the table, and Bull stared at him, wondering what had caused the sudden shift in energy. "Do you want to tell me another story?" Zach asked after taking another bite of his burger. He was obviously changing the subject, and Bull was more than happy to oblige.

"Mostly it's breaking up fights, especially after people have been drinking for a few hours. Of course, there are the guys who drink too much. Most nights we have someone pass out and we take them to the room I took you to, give them some coffee, and call them a cab. We want our patrons to be safe, and the bartenders watch for people drinking irresponsibly, but people buy drinks for others and the bartenders don't always see them." Bull chewed slowly and tried to think. "There was the time two drag queens went at it." Bull couldn't help grinning, and Zach smiled, some of the cloudiness in his expression now gone.

"You mean like a catfight?" Zach asked mirthfully.

"Sort of," Bull said, trying to curtail his laughter. "Apparently, this queen, Priscilla Delight, had been dating this guy for a while. Do you know Priscilla?" Zach shook his head. "She's thin, and I swear you'd never know she had boy parts under those dresses, complete with a chest you'd swear was real, but isn't. Anyway, Monica Glenn Ross is huge—two hundred pounds, with a voice that can stop traffic. Anyway, apparently Monica made a play for Priscilla's boyfriend, and Priscilla would have none of it. Feathers, hair from their wigs, bits of dress, you name it, were flying around the club before any of us could get there. The two of them were rolling on the floor, yelling, scratching at each other's eyes."

"Good God," Zach said, clearly entranced by the story.

Bull continued. "The thing was, by the time we broke them apart, big huge Monica was a mess, and Priscilla simply stood up and brushed herself off. That's one girl or guy you don't want to mess with. Apparently Priscilla knew how to fight and tore poor Monica to shreds. We kicked them both out and we had to pull them apart again when they started to go at it on the sidewalk." Bull sipped from his mug. "I can tell you, a woman scorned has nothing on a pissed-off drag queen."

"That's a good one," Zach told him as he finished writing and returned to his food. "That could have some great images: wigs, heels, and feathers flying."

They ate quietly for a while. It took Bull a few minutes to realize how comfortable he was. With people he didn't know well, he often examined them, wondering what their motivation was and how they were going to cause trouble. It was a hazard of his job... and his life. He didn't feel that at all now. It was nice just talking to Zach.

"Do you have any interesting stories about where you work?" Bull asked.

Zach shook his head. "I could tell you a Brantley story, I guess." Zach gulped some water from his glass. "Brantley is the most important person Brantley has ever met. He's a legend in his own mind." Zach swallowed, and Bull nodded. "So about three weeks ago, he gave me this assignment to design and prepare some ideas for a customer. Brantley hated everything I did. Finally, he drew out what he wanted on a piece of paper, and I made it up for him." Zach set down his water glass. "When the customer arrived, Brantley called me into his office, and we went over Brantley's idea for the account." Zach leaned over the table. "They hated it... bad." Zach scrunched his face like a little kid. "I had my tablet with me, so I thumbed through some other designs. They had me stop at one of the designs Brantley had hated. It was perfect for them and just what they wanted. I swear I could see the smoke coming out of Brantley's ears."

Bull snickered a little. He'd known people like Brantley—lots of them.

42

"He hemmed and hawed and actually kept pointing the client back to the design they hated. Finally, the top executive leaned over Brantley's desk and threatened to take his business elsewhere unless Brantley cleaned out his ears and effing listened." Zach grinned brightly. "I think that was the best day I ever had at work. The customer loved my design, and Brantley had to eat crow." Zach looked like he was doing a little happy dance in his seat. "I love what I do. I'm really creative, and I can come up with unique designs that customers really like. I just don't like working for my jerk of a boss. Kevin says not to worry. He thinks Brantley will either get fired or promoted soon. I'm voting for fired, but as long as I don't have to work with him any longer, I'll be really happy."

"He sounds like a real piece of work," Bull agreed. "I guess I'm lucky. Harry and I bought the club a few years ago, when the old owner was about to lose it. The police were about to shut him down because of all the troubles in the neighborhood, and once that happened he knew he'd never be able to open it. So he sold it to us, and we really cleaned house. Harry remodeled the inside, while I made sure no one got in who wasn't supposed to be there." Bull sighed. "That first year was tough. We had a lot of expenses and were turning people away because we had to clean out the undesirables. It took a few months for the word to get around that Bronco's was clean, and then we were in business."

"So you own the club, or part of it?" Zach asked, looking impressed.

"Yeah," Bull said. "In my former life I made quite a bit of money for a few years and was smart enough to save most of it. So when the opportunity came up, I had my share of the money. Harry and I have known each other since… it's hard for me to remember not knowing Harry. We were each other's firsts in a weird way." Bull paused and realized what he'd said. "We never slept together, but we told each other we were gay and sort of muddled through figuring out who we were together."

Bull flashed on memories of Harry and himself huddled together one summer evening in the tent in Harry's backyard when they were about fourteen. They had talked in whispers about what would happen if they were found out. At every sound they'd gotten quiet in case someone heard them. But they had each other. As kids, sometimes it was just the two of them, but that was all that mattered. As they grew up, they'd grown apart after high school, but they'd found each other again working at the same bar about six years ago.

Zach set down his fork. "It must have been nice to have someone to talk to about that." He sighed and then shrugged. "I had to figure everything out on my own, and once I did, it meant leaving my family."

"Where did you grow up?" Bull asked.

"Near Lancaster," Zach said, and Bull's mouth fell open. "I wasn't raised Amish, but my family is very conservative and religious. They would never understand." Zach cleared his throat. "They didn't understand, but they did their best. It was hard on all of us, especially coming from such a religiously based area where it seems everything is driven by what you and your neighbors believe."

"Did your family kick you out?" Bull asked with concern.

Zach shook his head. "Like I said, they tried to cope. But our neighbors didn't like it, and people at church looked at them suspiciously. So I stopped going to church, and eventually came here to go to school. I could still visit sometimes, but it was better for them if I was out of sight. After I graduated, I found a job and an apartment here."

"Didn't you meet people in college?"

"Yeah, but most of them live here in town. I didn't have what most people had for a college experience. I met some people, but often they moved on, so it wasn't like I made friends I had all four years."

"You were a loner, then?" Bull asked, and Zach nodded. Bull understood that. "What about the guys at the club?"

Zach grinned and the sadness disappeared. "I met them through Kevin, one of the guys I work with. He's really outgoing, and his circle of friends opened up to include me. They're a lot of fun." Zach picked up his hamburger. "I don't talk about myself very much. There's no need to bring everybody down." He took a bite and set the burger back on the plate. "I don't know why I'm telling you all this, except I feel like I can."

"Sometimes it's easier to tell things to a stranger," Bull said.

Zach nodded. "Can I ask you something? What's your real name?"

"Marvin Krebbs," Bull said. "Can you believe it? My mother named me Marvin. I always knew the woman hated me, and it started on the day I was born." Bull pushed the last bite of food onto his fork and stuffed it into his mouth. Then he sipped some of his coffee and sat back in the booth to relax. He was full and really satisfied. "So I go by Bull, and before you ask, you can't call me Marvin, or worse, Marv. I've been Bull for over twenty years and I like it that way."

Zach nodded, then blushed beet red and turned away.

"What?"

"I think Bull suits you. It's mysteriously sexy." Zach blushed harder, if that was possible. "Sorry, that was... God, I'm usually not forward like that."

"You didn't have a problem being forward at the club," Bull said. Zach was adorably cute when he blushed.

"I was with the guys and I'd already had a beer or two before we got there." Zach shrugged. "Isn't letting go something you're supposed to do at a club? I was having fun, and I didn't expect to see any of those people again. Besides, you really were tickling me."

Bull shook his head. He had nothing to say to that, and he figured he should be concentrating on the fact that Zach thought he was sexy. Bull pulled his libido back before he got carried away. He was here to talk to Zach about his comic book and to tell him stories about the club and have lunch. This wasn't a date. Bull stifled a groan. Zach sat across from him smiling happily, they'd just eaten, and Zach had actually told him he thought Bull was sexy. The only thing missing was a good-bye kiss. He signaled the server, and she brought the check. Bull reached for it before Zach could and handed her a twenty. There was enough for a tip, so he figured he could get up and leave anytime.

"What do you do when you aren't working at the club?" Zach inquired.

"Not much. I work when most people sleep, so I spend a lot of my days in bed. I used to play chess in a former life, but I haven't done that in years."

Damned if Zach didn't straighten right up. "I *love* chess. I used to play when I was in high school. We had a club, with all the nerdy kids, of course, and we used to meet once a week to challenge each other. I guess it was as close as I got to having friends for a while."

"I take it you weren't one of the popular kids?"

"Never was. I was too uptight, I guess. I mean, I knew I was different, but I didn't figure the whole thing out until—" Zach scratched his chin. "Well, I didn't actually admit the truth to myself until I was a senior in high school, but I knew and stayed away from most people in case they figured things out."

Bull understood that feeling really well. He supposed most gay kids did. At least he'd had Harry and they'd been able to go through all that stuff together. Bull was about to stand up when his phone rang. He pulled it out of his pocket and groaned. Zach tilted his head slightly. "It's my mother," Bull said with a roll of his eyes. Against his better judgment, he answered it, figuring he had a good excuse to keep the call short and hopefully away from her usual subject. "Hello," he said.

"Hi, Marvin, it's your mother," she said. Of course it was, because for one thing no one else ever called him Marvin.

"Hi, Mom, what do you need?" he said. She only ever called when she wanted something.

"Is that any way to greet your mother?" she asked snippily. Bull knew almost immediately that he'd hit the nail on the head. "Can't I call just to say hello to my son?" Her tone softened instantly. "I haven't seen you in months. I was thinking of coming up for a visit."

Those few words sent ice running through Bull's veins, and he shivered in the stuffy diner. "You know I don't have a lot of time right now. I spend my evenings and nights at the club. During the day I sleep, so I wouldn't have a lot of time to spend with you."

"I could go to the club when you do," she said brightly. "It would be fun to dance with all those handsome guys." Somehow he doubted the fun would last very long for her. The guys would indeed dance with her, but she'd find out very quickly that they weren't going to give her what she really wanted.

"Mom, now really isn't a good time for a visit. In a few months when I can plan things, I'll take some time away and come down to see you." Bull swallowed hard and fuck-all if his leg didn't shake slightly. "I'm at lunch with a friend." He glanced at Zach and smiled, receiving one in return that sent his pulse racing. "He's an artist and I'm helping him with a project." He desperately wanted to get her off the phone. "Can I call you later?"

"Honey, I just want to see you and I won't be any trouble," she said, but Bull remembered the last time she came for a visit and knew that was a lie.

"Mom, what's going on?" Bull asked.

"Nothing. Is it so bad that I want to spend some time with my son?" she asked, applying a liberal coating of guilt.

"No, but you never visit or call unless something has happened or you want something," Bull said forcefully. "I know that and so do you. So please just tell me what's happened and what it is you want."

"I'm your mother," she gasped in what Bull knew was mock horror. He had the world's most unmaternal mother.

"I know," he said, his resolve beginning to waver. "But I still know you."

"Your stepfather left me," she said flatly. Bull looked up at the ceiling and rolled his eyes to heaven.

"Is this my fifth stepfather or my sixth? I can't remember," Bull sniped. He'd only met Jerry once, but he seemed like a good enough guy for someone a year younger than Bull. "Look, I have to go. I'll call you later."

"Wait. I need some money," she said before he could hang up.

47

"Sorry, Mom," he said. "I told you the last time that was it. You need to go out and get a job. I can't continue to support you between stepfathers." Bull actually grinned at that remark.

"But...."

"We've already talked about this," Bull said evenly, keeping his anger in check. It would have been one thing if she were retired and living on a fixed income. He could see helping her then, but his mother was in her midfifties and she didn't want to work. "I gotta go," he added hurriedly. Then he said good-bye and hung up.

"Your mother," Zach said.

Bull nodded and took a deep breath. "Yeah, she wants money, as usual." He sighed. "She's also decided she wants to come for a visit."

"That's great," Zach said. "Isn't it?"

Bull shook his head. "I wish it were." Bull slid out of the booth and stood up, waiting for Zach to gather his things.

"Thank you for lunch and the stories. I really appreciate it," Zach told him quickly, as if the light had gone out of their conversation. Bull knew it was his fault. His mother could suck the brightness and fun out of any room, at least the ones he was in.

"You're welcome," Bull told him, forcing a smile. "I'm glad I could help, and your drawings are really great. I'm sure that once you get the book done, it will be a big success." They walked toward the door, where Bull waited so Zach could go first.

They stepped out onto the sidewalk and into the glorious summer sunshine and warmth. "Thanks again," Zach said, standing still for a few seconds, staring at him. Zach then held his sketchpads a little tighter to his chest, almost like they were a shield, before turning and walking away. Bull watched him go and then headed the other way. He'd only gone half a block before he stopped and swore under his breath. He was a complete idiot, and it served him right that he was going to spend another day off alone. Zach probably had plans, but.... Bull checked his watch. They'd spent well over an hour together and it had felt like only a few minutes. It was too late to do anything about it now, though, so he headed toward his car.

CHAPTER
FOUR

ZACH REACHED the corner and turned to look back at Bull, who was still standing in front of the diner. He'd been a dope to hope that Bull might ask to go somewhere or do something with him. Talking to him had been fun, and the time had flown by. He should have known a guy like Bull wouldn't notice a geeky kid like him. He'd done everything he could think of, including making a fool out of himself with the remark about Bull being sexy. His cheeks burned as he remembered it. Bull must have thought he was a real doofus. He looked away and turned the corner, then walked down the cobbled sidewalk to his car. Zach unlocked it and set his sketchbooks on the seat. He had nothing to do for the rest of the day, so he closed and locked the door before walking the block to Riverfront Park. Maybe some fresh air would make him feel better.

Zach loved Harrisburg's location on the bank of the Susquehanna River, which was wide and relatively shallow most of the time. Because the river could rise quickly from spring melt or heavy rain, the area directly adjacent to the river was a park. It wasn't very wide, but it ran for miles along the river, with large trees, walking paths, benches, and plenty of open, green, quiet space. Zach began walking north along the main path, which alternated between sun and shade. The walking bridge out to one of the islands in the river passed overhead. Zach had walked this area many times and gave no thought to continuing along the path.

"Gimme your money," Zach heard from behind him. His first instinct was to run, but something pressed to his side, and he stilled.

"I only got ten bucks," Zach said, realizing he was about to lose his extra fun money for the week. He reached into his pocket and pulled out his wallet, then handed the guy what he had. He didn't have credit cards or anything else of value with him.

"Fucking cheap bastard," the guy said. The object at his side pressed harder and then disappeared. The next thing Zach heard was footsteps. When he dared look around, he was alone. His knees buckled and he managed to get to a nearby bench before he collapsed. Just his luck to get robbed.

"Zach, you okay?" He looked up to see Bull kneeling beside the bench. "What happened?"

"I was robbed," Zach managed to gasp between short, nearly panicked breaths.

"Did he get much?" Bull asked.

Zach shook his head. "Just a few dollars." And his pride. "How could I be so stupid?"

"You weren't stupid. You gave him what he wanted, and he's gone." Bull lightly stroked Zach's arm. "He didn't hurt you, did he?"

"No. He just scared me," Zach said, and then he took a deep breath to try to stop his heart from pounding. "What are you doing here?"

"I come here sometimes when I want to think. I was taking a walk when I saw a guy run away, and then you nearly collapsed. I wasn't sure it was you at first." Bull sounded worried. "Do you think you can stand up?"

Zach breathed deeply and got to his feet. "I'm okay now. God knows I've been through a lot worse than someone stealing ten dollars. I thought he was going to hurt me because I didn't have more money."

"He most likely wanted to get away as quick as possible. Robbing people in broad daylight is pretty brazen and desperate."

"Scary too," Zach added as Bull took his arm. Zach turned to look at him and nearly gasped at the concern in Bull's eyes. "What?"

"I think this is the third or fourth time I've rescued you," Bull told him with an unreadable grin. "I guess third—twice at the club and once here."

"Well, technically, you didn't rescue me here, because he still got my money," Zach said.

"You must be feeling better if you can tease," Bull said.

Zach took a deep breath. "Yeah, well, who's going to try anything with you next to me?" Zach shifted his gaze upward, and Bull nodded. He stopped walking and tugged Bull to a halt. "You can smile sometimes. You did at the restaurant." Bull simply looked at him. "It improves your face value." Bull smiled and then groaned. "You know that movie." Bull growled again, but Zach had him. "No gay man can resist *Steel Magnolias.*" Zach cleared his throat. "The only thing that separates us from the animals is our ability to accessorize," he quoted in his best Southern accent, and that time Bull did indeed smile.

"That's so bad," Bull told him, and this time he chuckled.

"I can do Sally Field too," Zach said, the mugging momentarily slipping from his immediate memory. "I wanna know why!" he said, waving his arms, and Bull let go with a full-on belly laugh. Dang, that sound was hot. "You know, it's a little nellie that you actually know about this."

"No, it's not. I'm just older than you," Bull retorted, and Zach let it go. Their mutual mirth faded, and Zach's thoughts returned to the robbery.

"Should I call the police? They should probably know someone is robbing people in the park."

"They probably already do. He only got ten bucks," Bull said. "But you have to do what you feel is right. Even if you didn't file a report, you could call if you want."

"Is it worth it?" Zach asked. It was a small amount and he hadn't seen the guy, so it wasn't like anyone was going to catch him based on Zach's report. "Did you see him?"

"Not close enough to make a difference," Bull answered, and Zach sighed. "Let me see you back to your car."

"Okay, thanks," Zach agreed, and they turned around. Back at his car, he checked around to make sure all his stuff was still there before unlocking the door. "I really appreciate your help."

"I'm just angry I didn't arrive sooner," Bull said.

"I thought you were heading to your car." Zach pulled open his door, then paused before getting into the car.

"I like to walk in the park when I need to think."

"Me too. Or at least I used to. Next time I'll make sure I'm not alone when I do it." Zach slid into his seat and was about to close the door when Bull pulled out his wallet. He found a business card and handed it to him. "Call me if you like. We could have lunch again or something."

Zach took the card, a little unsure about the veracity of the invitation. But then maybe it was a stretch for Bull to extend the invitation at all. He wasn't the most approachable guy, that was for sure. "I'd like to have lunch again with you too." Zach pulled the door closed and waited until Bull moved away from the car before pulling into traffic.

"YOU HAD lunch with him?" Kevin asked. "I'm coming over, and you have to tell me all about it."

"There isn't much to tell," Zach said and waited for a response that never came. He looked at his phone, the call timer flashing. He turned it off and set the phone on the table beside his secondhand sofa. After about fifteen minutes spent watching television, Zach heard Kevin knocking on the door and got up to let him in. "What took you so long?"

"I got here as fast as I could," Kevin said as he sat on the other end of the sofa. "So what happened?"

"We just talked. I tried to tell you on the phone. We talked about the comic book, and he told me some stories. After lunch I went for a walk in the park and got mugged, and he was there to help me." Zach waited for Kevin's reaction, which was just as dramatic as he expected.

"You got *mugged*?" Kevin jumped closer. "You're okay? You didn't get hurt? Did you call the police? What did they say?"

Zach held up his hands. "Hold on. I'm fine. The mugger got the ten dollars I had in my wallet. I was scared half to death, but Bull showed up and made sure I was okay. He was really sweet about it. Then he gave me his card and said if I wanted, I could call him… for lunch." He stood and pulled the card out of his pocket, holding it out for Kevin to see. "I think he was just being nice."

"I don't," Kevin told him, practically bouncing on the sofa. "I think you should call him. But not today. Give him a day or so—you don't want to appear desperate—and then call him. That is, if you want to have lunch with him." Kevin paused. "Doesn't he seem kinda scary? I mean, the guy's huge, and…."

"He's really nice," Zach said.

Kevin appeared skeptical. "He probably just wants to get in your pants. Not like that's a bad thing, but I checked around at the club. A friend said that he went home with Bull once, a few years ago. Apparently Bull's built like his name, but he doesn't do commitment of any kind. My friend Sam said he has never seen Bull with the same guy twice. Not that he really takes them anywhere except home to bed."

"Do you think a guy like Bull would really want to take me home to bed?" Zach asked. He knew what he looked like. He'd taken the time to look at himself naked more than once. Sure, he had some nice parts, but the whole package wasn't anything great to look at. "Get real, Kevin." Zach stood up. "He gave me his number and said I could call him for lunch. He didn't ask me back to his place or anything." Zach shook his head. It was easier to get angry at Kevin than let his disappointment show through.

"Hey, I'm sorry to burst your bubble," Kevin said.

"You didn't, not really," Zach confessed. He shoved the card back into his pocket. "It was nice to talk to him, and he was really kind in the park. I know he was probably doing what he'd do with anyone, but it was a nice illusion."

Kevin pulled him back down onto the sofa and sat next to him. "I'm sorry I said anything. I thought you should know what I found out, but I probably should have kept my big mouth shut."

"Why?" Zach asked.

"Because now you probably won't call him, and I think you should. I didn't want you to get your hopes up, but it also could be different. I saw the way he kept looking at you at the club. The big guy couldn't take his eyes off you." Kevin settled back against the cushions.

"Then why didn't you say anything last night?"

"Because I thought you knew. He kept watching our table. Every time you laughed, he was watching. I thought, him being a bouncer, he thought we might have been up to something, but now I think he was watching you."

"So what do I do?" Zach asked, pulling out the card again. "Should I call him or not?"

"In a few days. If you say who you are and he's excited to hear from you, then that's a good sign. But if he can't remember who you are, then forget about him and move on," Kevin told him seriously. Zach sat and watched Kevin for a few seconds. "What?"

"If you know so much about getting a date and going out with guys, then why do you spend every weekend with me? You certainly aren't going to get any." Zach jumped up as Kevin lunged for him. He laughed as he raced toward the bedroom. A throw pillow sailed past his head. Zach scooped it up and lobbed it back at Kevin, hitting him square in the chest. "So when was the last time you were out on a date?"

"I've got one for Friday night, if you must know," Kevin told him. Zach stopped and walked back to the sofa, throwing the pillow against the arm. "I met him while you and the big guy were talking. His name's Louie, and I've seen him around the club a few times. We've talked, and he asked me out last night. Since most guys are there looking to hook up, I'm excited he actually asked me out instead of just to go into the bathrooms or something."

"Do guys really do that?"

"Yeah. The bathrooms are one of the hookup spots. Those stalls have seen tons of action. But no one goes near them if Bull's around, though. I heard a few weeks ago he dumped cold water on a couple of guys who were trying to get busy." Kevin laughed. "Apparently the screams could be heard all the way to the dance floor."

SOMEHOW ZACH managed to wait until Tuesday afternoon on his coffee break before trying to call Bull. His hand shook a little as he dialed the number on the card. He'd spent the past two days deciding between making the call and throwing the card away because he figured he was being a complete idiot. In the end, he decided it was only a phone call and it would be dumb not to try. He waited for the call to connect.

"Hello," Bull said.

"Umm," Zach began. "This is…." A crash sounded in the background and Bull swore under his breath.

"Can you hold on a minute?" Bull asked, and then a thud sounded as the phone was set down. Zach waited and heard a few more crashes, smiling when he realized they were pots and pans as opposed to something worse. "Dang cupboard shelf decided to go."

"Umm, this is Zach," he said once he thought Bull was listening.

"Zach." The excitement in Bull's voice was unmistakable. "I was hoping you'd call."

He swallowed. "I wasn't sure you really wanted me to. Since you gave me the card I hoped you were sincere, but I wasn't sure because after the whole.... Sorry, I'm rambling," he said, and then he paused to take a breath. "I tend to do that when I get nervous."

"Just so you know, I never give anyone a card with my personal number on it that I don't want to call." He heard Bull sigh. "And I was hoping you'd call."

"You had said we could get together for lunch. I have to work during the week and only get half an hour...."

"For me, lunch is at your dinnertime, so I'd like to take you out to dinner," Bull said, and Zach's stomach did a little flip-flop.

"Is this, like, a date?" Zach asked tentatively. What Kevin had told him about Bull had been running through his mind for days, and he'd finally come to the conclusion that if Bull was only interested in a quickie, then he'd say no thank you and move on. Zach knew he was young, but he wanted to find love—to be in love. Yeah, he wanted to have sex, but he didn't think he wanted to just have sex. His thoughts got all messed up, especially at night when he jerked off thinking about Bull.

"No, it's not *like* a date," Bull said.

"Oh...," Zach muttered.

"It *is* a date," Bull clarified, and Zach laughed. "I want to take you on a dinner date. You'll have to bear with me because it's been a long time since I went out on a real date. Mostly lately...." Bull paused briefly, and Zach waited. "I haven't met anyone I wanted to date in a while."

"Why not?"

Bull didn't answer right away, and Zach wondered if he'd crossed some kind of line. "How about I tell you that when I see you?" Bull was hedging; Zach could feel it.

"You don't have to tell me anything you don't want to," Zach said. Lord knew he had plenty of stuff he didn't like to talk about.

"Okay. Are you free Thursday night? About six o'clock? I could pick you up if you give me your address."

Zach smiled. "Thursday would be nice." He gave Bull his address along with his phone number. "Do you have to work tonight?"

"No," Bull answered. "I usually have Monday and Tuesday nights off. I've decided to take Thursday this week so I can have the evening with you, but that's unusual. Friday and Saturday nights are impossible. Unless there's an emergency, I always work those nights."

"I can understand that," Zach said. He glanced at the clock and realized he needed to get back to work. "I have to go or I'll be in trouble, but I'm glad I called, and I'll see you Thursday at six." They said good-bye, and then Zach hung up, left the breakroom, and walked back to his desk.

"Did you call him?" Kevin whispered as he poked his head around the cubicle partition.

"Yeah," Zach whispered and pumped his hand in the air before breaking into a grin. "Thursday for dinner," he added before returning to work in case Brantley caught him. He tried to keep his excitement in check, but it was most definitely difficult, and he wondered how he would make it through the next two days.

HE DID, somehow. Thursday afternoon, Zach got out of work on time and rushed home. Almost as soon as he stepped into his apartment, his phone rang. Of course it was Kevin. "He's picking me up at six," Zach said before Kevin could ask. "What I don't understand is why my date is so important to you."

"You're my friend, and I want you to be happy. No one I know deserves to be happy more than you." There was something unusual in Kevin's tone.

"What is it you aren't saying?" Zach asked as he pulled open his closet door and started looking for something nice to wear, thumbing through the hangers. He was by no means a clotheshorse.

"Nothing at all. I just want to make sure you have a good time." Kevin went quiet for a while, then said, "I guess I'm a little worried. He's so big, and his reputation…. What if he hurts you or something?"

"He's taking me to dinner at a restaurant." Zach's mind drifted back to the night Bull had rescued him—twice—at the club. "I think everyone has him wrong or at least *might* have him wrong. The few times Bull has touched me, he's been nothing but gentle and caring."

"So you're saying he's a pussycat on the inside," Kevin remarked skeptically.

"I don't know if I'd say that. But I find him attractive and interesting and I'm comfortable around him. Or as comfortable as anyone can be when they're talking to a guy the size of a brick outhouse." Zach chuckled.

"What if he is the way everyone else says?" Kevin asked.

"Then I'll call you to come get me," Zach told him. "I promise on a stack of Bibles." Somewhere deep inside he knew it wouldn't come to that. He had little idea why other than the way Bull had treated him. Yes, the guy was intimidating as all hell, there was no doubt about it, but there was something else too. Zach paused and sat on the edge of the bed. "You're going to think I'm really stupid, but when we were at lunch the other day, Bull's mother called, and after he hung up, I saw… something in his expression."

"O-kay," Kevin drawled skeptically.

Zach chose to ignore it. "The thing is, it was an expression I've seen more than once when I've looked at myself in the mirror." Kevin scoffed softly. "I know, and maybe I'm seeing things, but maybe he's been through the same kind of hell I've been through." Zach checked his watch and jumped up. "I gotta go, but I'll have my phone with me and I promise to call if he so much as hints that he's after my virtue." He knew Kevin was rolling his eyes as they disconnected. Zach hurried back to his closet and hunted down a pair of dress slacks. They were a few years old, but thankfully they still fit. He found a shirt to go with them and changed clothes in a hurry. Then he rushed into the bathroom and brushed his teeth,

58

wanting to have clean breath. He also splashed on a little cologne. When he was done, he checked his reflection in the mirror and left the bedroom as a knock sounded on his door.

He hurried to the door and pulled it open. "You're a little early, but I'm almost ready." Zach stared at the man on the other side of his door. "What are you doing here?" He slipped his hand in his pocket, clutching his phone in case he needed to call for help.

"Is that any way to speak to family?" his Uncle Hiram said as he stepped into the apartment.

"I'm sorry, but all of you turned your back on me some time ago," Zach said. *Why is he here and what does he want?* "So I'll ask again: What are you doing here?"

"I was in town and got your address from the Internet. I thought I'd stop in and see how you were doing." His uncle looked around the room, and Zach saw it the way he probably was seeing it—the old, mismatched furniture, bookshelves cobbled together from bricks and planks of wood, the secondhand rug that covered the scuffed floor. "Obviously not very well." He turned to Zach. "You know, if you gave up this deviant lifestyle, you could return to the family."

"Uncle Hiram, I am who I am and I like the life I've built for myself," Zach said nervously. His uncle was the head of the family, and the values Zach had been raised with died hard. His parents had deferred to Uncle Hiram for important decisions, and that training still existed inside him. "I'm not interested in returning, so you don't have to worry about me embarrassing you or the family. I have a life here and I take care of myself. I won't be calling to ask for anything, and I expect the same courtesy from you."

"That is no way to speak to your elders and betters," his uncle said forcefully and stepped forward. Zach's instinct was to back down, but he suppressed it and stood firm.

"You turned your back on me, remember? When you did that, you stepped out of my life, and in a weird way freed me from your overbearing control." His uncle raised his hand. "Don't you dare," Zach challenged. "I'm not a child, and any physical abuse will result in me calling the police. This isn't Townsend, where you have everyone in your back pocket."

His uncle was speechless for a few seconds. "I told your aunt this was a useless errand, but she insisted I see you while I was here to try to talk some sense into you. It seems since your departure, other young people are looking to leave the family."

A knock sounded on the doorframe, and then Bull said, "Am I interrupting anything?"

"No," Zach told Bull with a smile. "My uncle was just leaving." He watched as his uncle turned and saw Bull, and he saw his uncle's eyes widen. "Unless you want to discuss things further with my boyfriend, I suggest you go, Uncle Hiram." Zach knew he was taking a chance, and he hoped Bull would understand and let him stretch the truth. They were hardly boyfriends, but Zach needed the illusion of strength—that was all his uncle understood. Bless his heart, Bull growled and stepped forward. Zach watched as his uncle warily stepped around Bull and then left the apartment without another word.

"What was that about?"

"My father's older brother. He's the patriarch of my family." Zach glanced around and stepped closer to Bull. "I'm ready to go when you are."

Bull glared at him. "He looked like he was about to hit you," he said almost accusingly.

"He probably was. Uncle Hiram was always a bully. When I was a kid, I lived in fear of him, and that was what he wanted. All the kids did what he wanted, and that carried right on into adulthood."

"Sounds like some sort of cult," Bull observed, crossing his arms over his chest.

"It's just very old-fashioned and conservative, or at least that's how it started. But I think my uncle runs the family like his own little fiefdom. The land my family farms is owned by the entire family, in some sort of trust. No one owns their own part of it, and Uncle Hiram is the leader, so what he says goes," Zach explained. "I told you my folks tried to understand me, but the people in the community turned their backs—well, that was led by my uncle."

"Where are your parents now? Do they still live there?" Bull asked.

"No. The house I grew up in burned to the ground with them inside less than a year after I left home." Zach swallowed and turned away, trying to wipe his eyes so Bull wouldn't see. The loss of his parents still really hurt. "Most of the people back home turned their backs, but my parents still loved me. I know that. They came to visit me a few times, but it was hard on them. I know they didn't understand my being gay and that it hurt them, but they still tried. What I don't understand is why my uncle was so angry and hurtful." Zach caught his breath and stopped himself from blubbering for the millionth time since he'd gotten the news.

"I'm sorry," Bull said, and Zach saw he really understood. The sadness Zach felt on a regular basis was mirrored back at him.

"The sucky part was no one bothered to tell me until after the funeral. I got a call from one of my parents' friends and she told me what had happened. My uncle couldn't be bothered. Mrs. Phillips, the woman who called me, she said my uncle was afraid I'd disrupt the solemnity of the funeral or something." Zach swallowed really hard. "I think the old goat envisioned me jumping on the tables at the luncheon and doing a striptease." Zach began to laugh, and then he couldn't stop. He laughed until tears came to his eyes. Then he felt Bull put his arms around him and hold him, and he buried his face against Bull's chest.

The dam burst, and he began to sob. He knew this was a terrible idea, and dang it, he'd cried enough over the loss of his folks, but he couldn't help it. When Mrs. Phillips had called to tell him about his parents' death, Zach had been alone and at school. There had been no one he could turn to, or at least no one he felt comfortable turning to, so he'd dealt with it as best he could on his own. And he'd been doing that same thing ever since. "I'm so sorry," he mumbled wetly. He had to be getting Bull's shirt wrinkled and damp. "You look so nice, and I'm messing you all up." Zach moved to step away, but Bull held him tighter. Zach lightly stroked Bull's chest. "You dressed up for me, didn't you? I always see you in black jeans and a black T-shirt, but you dressed up for me."

"I wanted you to have a nice evening," Bull said without letting him go. "You know, this is really nice. Like, it feels right to hold you like this."

Zach wiped his eyes and sniffed. Bull let his hands fall to his sides, and Zach stepped back. "Maybe we should go." He felt like a sniveling idiot—not the impression he wanted to make. "I drooled on your shirt." Zach hurried to the kitchen and returned with a towel. He used it to help dry Bull's shirt. "Sorry about the mess."

Bull took his hand, stopping it midwipe. "It's okay. It's only a shirt." Bull tugged him closer, and Zach lifted his gaze. Bull slowly moved nearer, and Zach tilted his head, his eyes sliding closed. He braced himself, and within seconds, Bull lightly kissed him. Then Bull held him close and kissed him again. Zach moaned softly, and Bull deepened the kiss further for just a few seconds. Then he gentled it and pulled his lips away.

Zach opened his eyes and blinked a few times, wondering if this was real. Had Bull just kissed him? He stared into Bull's deep-green eyes and smiled. It *was* real and not some weird trick of his imagination. He'd imagined those eyes staring into his and Bull's lips on his so many times. But this had been nothing like he'd imagined—it was so much better. "You kissed me." God, he sounded stupid.

"Yes, I did," Bull whispered. Zach smiled and closed his eyes, resting his head on Bull's chest.

"I won't drool this time, I promise."

Bull laughed, his chest vibrating with what sounded to Zach like deep happiness. "You can drool on me anytime you like." Bull lightly wrapped his arms around Zach's shoulders. "How about we go to dinner? I'm really hungry."

"Okay," Zach agreed, but neither of them made a move.

"Why did your uncle show up now?" Bull asked. Zach shrugged. His uncle had given him some lame excuse about his aunt, but Zach knew that was bullsquirt. "Do you think he'll hang around?"

"No." Zach answered softly. "He'll go home and terrorize the locals."

"Did they ever figure out why your parents' home burned down?"

"They said it was faulty wiring or something like that. I think it was just an excuse because my parents weren't really interested in doing what Uncle Hiram wanted them to."

"He really has that kind of power?" Bull asked.

Zach stepped back. "Uncle Hiram controls the largest plot of land in the county. That brings in a lot of money, so, yeah. Everyone does what my uncle says back home. If he lived in New York, he'd be, like, the godfather. Maybe what pisses him off is that I got out. I'm one less person under his thumb. I really don't care any longer. He lives sixty miles away and he's welcome to do what he wants. I don't visit anymore or talk to anyone from back home." Zach gave Bull a half smile. "I'm on my own now, and I think I really like being able to make my own decisions."

I suppose you do," Bull said softly. "I understand what it feels like to have others making your decisions for you." Bull sighed. "I didn't like it either." He stepped back and cleared his throat slightly. "Let's go to dinner." He moved toward the door, and Zach checked that he had his keys and wallet before following him out and locking the apartment. Then he followed Bull outside to his car. Zach stared at the powder-blue convertible and whistled softly. "This is really nice."

"It's a '65 Mustang," he said. "I keep it in the garage and only drive it on special occasions. It was my dad's, and it's one of the few things I have from him." Bull leaned over and opened the door. "He never drove it much, and after he died, it was specifically left in his will to me." Zach slid into the seat and pulled the door closed. "There were so many times when I was younger that I thought of selling it. I needed the money so bad I could barely stand it. But I held on to it because it was my dad's, and because once it was gone, it would be gone forever and I'd never find another one." Bull started the engine and it roared to life, sending vibrations of power through the car and into the seat.

"Wow," Zach said, looking over at Bull. "This thing has power."

"Lots of it, but I promise to take it easy." Bull backed out of the parking space and drove slowly away from Zach's building. "I wasn't sure what you liked, so I planned on eating at Black and Bleu. They have a good variety."

"Sounds nice," Zach said. He'd seen the place but had never stopped. He didn't go out for dinner much because he really couldn't afford anything other than when the guys came over and they ordered a pizza or something.

He rested his arm on top of the door and sat back, letting the sun and warm air caress his face. "Can I ask what you did before you bought the club?" Zach inquired when they stopped at one of the traffic lights.

Bull glanced over, and Zach saw him grip the wheel tighter. "I was a mercenary." Bull turned his gaze forward, and when the light changed color, he punched the accelerator and they jumped forward, speeding down the road. Zach didn't quite know what to say or exactly what Bull meant. He knew a mercenary was a soldier for hire, but did that mean Bull had hired himself out to kill people? He sat silently and stared out the windshield. Bull pulled into the parking lot of the restaurant, found a place well away from the other parked cars, and turned off the engine, but didn't move.

"What does that mean?" Zach asked. "Were you hired to kill people?"

"I'm not an assassin," Bull said. "After high school I went into the military and qualified for a special unit. It was our job to go in and take care of problems that no one wanted on the evening news. We got in and out and no one knew we'd been there. After I was discharged, I was contacted about private work. My skills were in demand, and I worked for a number of people who required special protection."

"Oh, sort of like a security guard?"

Bull cleared his throat. "No. These were people who definitely had other people who wanted them dead, high-profile people who others were out to kill. It was my job to see to it that they stayed alive. I can't give you details because that's part of the deal. They don't talk about me, and I don't talk about them." Bull shifted in the seat. "If you want, I can take you home. What I did makes a lot of people uncomfortable, so I would understand."

"You don't do that sort of stuff now?" Zach asked, and Bull shook his head. "You didn't kill innocent people or hurt someone who wasn't out to get you?"

"No," Bull said. "I'm not a murderer. I did some things that others might not be happy about or think were necessarily aboveboard, but it was part of the job, and I was good at it. Hell, I loved it, but after a while I couldn't do it any longer."

"I'm glad you told me," Zach said. "I take it you don't tell many people." Bull shook his head, and Zach leaned over to him. "I'd say I understand, but I really don't. I suppose it's one of those things you had to be there for." Zach touched Bull's chin, and he turned toward him. Without saying anything more, Zach leaned close and kissed Bull on the lips right there in the parking lot with the top down. People could see, but he didn't really care.

"What would your uncle think if he saw what you just did?" Bull asked and then grinned.

Zach laughed hard. "He'd probably have sputtered and choked as he swallowed his false teeth." He reached for the door handle and then paused. "Maybe we should find him and give him a command performance. I bet he'd never come within a hundred miles of me again." Zach continued laughing and thought about the look on his uncle's pinched face. He'd probably look like he'd been sucking a lemon.

"So you're okay with this?" Bull asked.

"Why wouldn't I be? It was your job." Zach said, even though the thought was both hot and gave him pause. "I always knew you were dangerous, but in a good way."

65

Bull opened his door and got out of the car. He walked around the back and waited for Zach to join him. "How can I be dangerous in a good way?"

"Well, you're strong. You could probably snap me like a twig if you wanted. But you don't," Zach said. "Do you remember when you lifted me out of the crowd of people? You picked me up off the floor and carried me away from danger, and you did it with such care. You were gentle. You could have been heavy-handed, but you weren't. And that's what I mean, I guess. You have all this strength and power, but you don't use it unless you have to. At least you didn't with me."

They reached the door of the restaurant, and Bull held it open for him. "I don't get it. Most people take one look at me and either back away or they're the slave submissive types who think I'd be the daddy they've spent all their lives trying to find. What did I do that made you see something different? If you tell me, then I'll be sure not to do it again."

"Har har," Zach said, trying to cover for the fact that the only answer he had for that question wasn't much of an answer at all. "The only thing I can tell you is that I get the feeling we aren't all that different."

Bull raised his eyebrows in surprise and looked down at himself and then at Zach. "I don't see it."

"Maybe because in this case, the similarities aren't on the surface," Zach said. He could tell Bull wasn't convinced, but he saw it, or at least thought he did. Before he could say anything more, Bull stepped up to the podium and gave his name for the reservation. The hostess reached for menus and led them through the restaurant to a table off to one side. They had a nice view of the dining room, and Zach took his seat and waited for Bull to do the same. "Have you been here before?"

"Yes, a few months ago. They have great steaks and wonderful pasta dishes. I haven't had anything else, but most things are quite good," Bull said. They opened their menus and looked them over while a busboy filled their water glasses. The server then stopped by, introduced herself, and took their drink and appetizer orders.

"You said you hadn't been on a date in a while," Zach said. He felt he needed to keep the conversation going.

"No. My social life lately has consisted of bringing guys home for—well, let's say most of them didn't stay the night. Because I rarely let them. The few who did left in the morning, and I promptly forgot them." Bull reached for his water. "I don't let people get close to me. Since I left the job as a mercenary, I haven't let anyone into my life."

"Then why are you letting me?" Zach asked. "Or is this just a prelude to what you hope will be another of those one-night stands? Because that isn't what I want. I deserve better than that."

"No. That's not why we're here," Bull said and then turned toward the server as their appetizers and drinks were set on the table. She took their entree orders and then left them alone.

Zach took an onion ring and let it cool before taking a bite. He waited to see if Bull would give more of an explanation, but nothing seemed forthcoming. "So... why are we here?"

"You don't believe in cutting a guy any slack, do you?"

"Nope," Zach answered. "But if it makes you feel better, I haven't been on many dates either. Well, to be exact, I've been on one date before. It didn't go very well. He figured he could buy me dinner, a few drinks, and then that gave him the right to do what he wanted." Bull narrowed his eyes. "He didn't get what he wanted and went home with a case of very sore balls from where I kneed him when he wouldn't take no for an answer. So whatever nervousness you're feeling, I'm going through the exact same thing." Zach reached for his water, and Bull mirrored the action, but didn't offer any more to the conversation.

Zach wasn't sure what else to do. Conversation seemed like pulling teeth, and he wasn't sure what other topics to bring up. Bull didn't seem to want to talk about himself, and Zach wasn't really up to talking about his past or his family. He'd done that once already, and the drool stain on Bull's shirt was only now drying. Zach shifted his gaze to the table and picked up another onion ring. He nibbled at it and tried to think of something to talk about. Maybe he and Bull didn't have as much in common as he'd thought. They barely knew each other, and Zach realized he might have been projecting his own feelings and emotions onto Bull.

"Do you like sports?" Bull asked him.

"Not really. I used to play soccer when I was a kid, but I was terrible. My mom drove me to the field every Saturday for months, and most of the time I sat on the bench and watched. I guess that should have been a clue to everyone about the kind of guy I was. Eventually I was put into the game. The ball came at me, and I ran up to it to kick as hard as I could." Zach paused, remembering like it was yesterday. "I kicked and fell on my back, completely missing the ball. That was the end of my soccer career. I'm not good with balls."

Bull began to laugh. "How do you know?"

Zach stared for a second and then he got it. He smiled and then laughed right along with Bull. "I guess I don't know yet." His laughter faded. "Were you good at sports?"

"God, yes. I played everything when I was a kid: football, basketball, some baseball. I was really good at football. I was always a big kid, so football really fit. Basketball was great until high school. Then I really filled out, and that counteracted my height. My dad had hopes that I'd play professional football. He died when I was still in high school, and a few years later, my mother started the never-ending parade of stepfathers. As soon as I graduated high school, I enlisted in the army. College wasn't for me, I knew that for sure, and I needed a job. The military gave me that, and then I discovered some skills and talents I hadn't realized I had. I'd never shot a gun before, but I turned out to have a natural ability for marksmanship and quickly developed spot-on aim. I also found I had a mind for strategy and counterstrategy. When planning a mission, I could think many moves ahead of the others. If something happened, I'd almost always already thought about it and had a plan in place to deal with it." The server brought their food, and Bull quieted until she left. "After that, I started planning and leading missions. That was a big part of my life, though I still can't talk about any of the details."

"I suppose there are lots of things you can't talk about," Zach said as he took a small bite of his pasta. Bull had been right about the food. He closed his eyes as the tangy, rich sauce coated his tongue. After he swallowed, he heard a small groan. When Zach opened his eyes, he saw Bull staring back at him, his mouth slightly open.

"It's good?" Bull asked. "Because, damn... the way you looked...." Bull leaned over the table, and Zach saw him shiver.

"Yes, it's really good. Some of the best I've ever had," Zach said. "Do you want some?" He put some pasta on his fork. Bull opened his mouth, and Zach slipped the fork between his lips. Bull chewed and smiled.

"It is good, but I really like watching you eat it." Bull's eyes danced, and Zach wondered if he should be self-conscious. He looked down at the table. "Hey," Bull said. "Watching you with that pasta was sexy as hell. I love how you throw yourself into whatever you like. Whether it's dancing, your drawings, or enjoying your food, you immerse yourself in what you do. That's attractive."

"I didn't know I was doing anything," Zach said.

"You were just being yourself," Bull told him.

"Well, most of the time, being myself wasn't good enough," Zach said. Too many times the other kids, even some of the adults around him, had made it plain he didn't measure up or fit in.

"It's good enough for me," Bull said. Zach nearly dropped his fork. "You don't have to be anything other than yourself. That's all that's required, and it's what I like." Bull returned to his food as though he hadn't just said what he'd said. And maybe he simply didn't realize what those words had meant to Zach. Very few people in his life had accepted him for who he was, and the most important of those people were gone. His parents probably hadn't understood, but they'd loved him and wanted him to be himself. His friends accepted him—at least he hoped they did. But to most of the other

69

people who'd been part of his life, Zach had been an embarrassment; he knew that. He still was. "What?" Bull asked after a few seconds, and Zach realized he'd been staring.

"Nothing," Zach said with a smile. "You made me happy. That's all."

"Good. I like making you happy." Bull took a bite of his steak.

"Why?" Zach took a small bite of pasta. "What's so special about me?"

"You really don't see it, do you?" Bull asked, and Zach shrugged. "You're not devious and you don't hide what you're feeling. You don't have ulterior motives when you ask a question. I've spent my entire adult life trying to figure out the motives behind everyone's actions. Some people are easy. Take my mother. She'll do anything so she can have as easy a life as possible. She's married three or four men since my dad died because they promised to take care of her. Whenever she calls, she wants money so she doesn't have to go out and earn it. She's happiest when she doesn't have to make decisions and has someone to simply handle everything in her life for her. She'll connive, lie, use guilt, anything she can, to get what she wants."

"Wow," Zach said under his breath. "Are you sure you aren't a little biased?"

"Probably," Bull said. "But dealing with her for so many years has left me with little tolerance for her. It wasn't like she was the most loving or caring mother. Before my dad died, she was different, happier, but afterwards, she got bitter and more self-absorbed."

"Okay," Zach began. "How about we talk about happier things? I think we've exhausted parents, previous jobs, and family." He set down his fork. "You know what I always wanted to do? Fly model airplanes. You know, the kind with the remote controls."

"I flew some of the real remote-control airplanes when I was in the military. They can be a lot of fun. Once, over...." Bull stopped and shook his head. "Are you really interested in flying model planes or did you just pick that out of the air?"

70

"It got us off the subject of family," Zach said with a grin. Bull laughed.

"That it did. Okay, we'll talk about fun things. How about afterwards we go dancing? I know a place where we can have the time of our lives."

"But today's your day off," Zach said. "Won't everyone at the club start asking you for things and expecting you to take charge and stuff?"

"I wasn't talking about the club," Bull said. Zach wasn't quite sure what he meant, but a little surge of electricity shot through him and he nodded before allowing any second thoughts.

They finished their meals, and Bull took the check and paid the waitress with a credit card. Then they left the table and went out to Bull's car. The evening was still warm and the fresh air felt great as they drove through town and then to a quiet residential area. Bull pulled into the drive of a small home and parked the car in the garage.

Zach got out, expecting Bull to lead him inside, but instead, Bull opened the gate and they went into the landscaped backyard. Zach looked around at the manicured green shrubs and large trellis with a swing beneath it.

"The people I bought the house from did an incredible job with the backyard." Bull seemed to remember something. "I'll be right back." He hurried into the garage and returned with a cushion he placed on the seat of the swing under the trellis. "Have a seat if you like." Bull motioned, and Zach sat down, then slowly rocked back and forth while Bull went inside.

When Bull returned this time, he had a bottle of wine and two glasses. He pulled up a small table and set them down. Then he sat next to Zach on the swing.

"It's very pretty and quiet back here," Zach said.

"It is," Bull said as he shifted on the swing. "You're the first person I've ever brought here. I love to sit here and enjoy the peace and quiet sometimes before I go to work." Bull lightly stroked Zach's cheek and then leaned in.

Zach held still with anticipation. Bull kissed him gently and then deepened it, wrapping Zach in his arms. He placed a hand on Bull's strong chest, lightly sucking on his lip. It was a nice kiss that quickly deepened into one that curled Zach's toes. Bull tasted sweeter than Zach had expected, and when he realized it and that he wanted more, he shifted on the swing, pressed himself to Bull, and took it.

Bull moaned when Zach thrust his tongue in Bull's mouth, tasting him deeply. Bull held him close, and within minutes, Zach felt as though he were floating on the combination of Bull's heady scent and rich sweet taste.

The sound of a throat clearing stopped him dead still. Zach pulled away and swallowed before turning to look in the direction of the sound. An older woman stood at the back door of the house, staring at the two of them. Bull groaned, and Zach's cheeks flamed as he straightened up and turned around to sit properly in the swing, wishing the ground would swallow him. "Who's that?" he asked softly.

"My mother."

CHAPTER FIVE

BULL STOOD up. "What are you doing here?" He glanced at a very confused and shocked-looking Zach before walking over to where his mother stood.

"I told you I was coming for a visit. You never called me back, so I got in the car and drove up to see you," she said as though it were the most normal thing in the world for her to drive twelve hundred miles just to visit him.

"I told you I was very busy," Bull ground between his teeth.

"I can see how busy you are. Now tell your little playmate to go home," she said.

"Excuse me, Mother, but this is my home, not yours. You weren't invited, so I really hope you made plans as to where you were going to stay," Bull said, knowing full well she had planned to move in with him for the duration of her visit.

"I'll stay with you, of course. I'm your mother." As though being his mother entitled her to anything and everything she wanted from him.

"How did you get in?"

"I have a key," she told him, holding up her key ring. For the life of him, Bull could not remember giving her one.

"I don't know what you're up to, but this ends now. I have plans and I need to work. This isn't a good time for you to be here."

Bull shook his head. His mother had just dropped in on him. Of course she knew, just as well as he did, that if she'd asked, he would have said no. So she simply hadn't asked. "You can stay a few days and then you need to drive right back home."

"Is that the welcome I get for coming all this way?"

"Uninvited," Bull clarified and stared at her. She stared back, and in the past that might have worked, but Bull was just angry enough that he continued staring until he saw her discomfort. "Like I said, you can drive back to Florida in a couple of days. Until then, if you cause trouble, you'll have to move to a hotel." He tried to keep his voice as even as possible, but he knew his mother was trouble. During and just after her last divorce, she'd drunk herself into near oblivion more than once and had probably done other things she either couldn't remember or refused to acknowledge.

"Bull," Zach said from behind him, and Bull turned, softening his gaze.

"Zach," Bull said, remembering the manners his mother had never taught him, "this is my mother, Charlene. Mom, this is Zach." He hated the way she'd referred to Zach earlier, and he glared at her in case she made another remark. They shook hands, but the tension emanating from his mother could have filled an ocean. "We had planned to spend the evening together," he explained as a nice way of telling her that she had interrupted.

"Well, I need to get settled and then eat something." She looked at him as if he was supposed to take care of that for her.

"You know where the guest room is, and there is a little food in the refrigerator. If you don't find something you like, there are restaurants a few blocks south on Market." He seethed inside that she'd disrupted his and Zach's time together.

"All right," she said, and then she turned around and went back into the house.

Bull took Zach by the hand and led him back over to the swing. "I'm sorry about all this. I had no idea she was coming. The last time we spoke was when she called me while we were having lunch last weekend."

"It's okay. She's your mother," Zach said with longing. "Maybe you should take me home so you can spend time with her. She drove a long way, even if she didn't tell you, and you should spend some time with her."

"I was hoping to spend the rest of the evening with you," Bull said, but that would be impossible now. His mother's appearance had sent all the plans he'd had for the rest of their evening up in smoke. "Let me make sure she's settled, and then I'll take you home." Maybe it was for the best.

He stood up and went inside. Bull found his mother in the guest room, unpacking her things. "Is he leaving?" she asked without turning around.

"I'm going to take him home," Bull said as he entered the room. "What the hell were you thinking coming here without so much as a call?"

"I'm your mother," she answered.

"That means nothing. After Dad died, you weren't much of anything to anyone except yourself. You can stay a few days, but then you're going back home."

"I need some time away so I can relax and try to think," she told him. Bull wasn't buying it, but he couldn't think of a counterargument right now.

"If you want something to eat, you can ride with Zach and me. We'll stop and get something when I take him home." Bull turned to leave, but stopped in the doorway. "But be nice to him."

"I'm always nice," she said with a smile.

"No, you're not. You've known I'm gay for years, but you refuse to accept it. Well, you will now or you'll go home. We haven't had much of a relationship in years, so I don't know why you expect one to sprout overnight simply because you don't want to be alone."

His mother turned and sat on the edge of the bed. "I don't know where else to turn."

"I know you don't. But dropping in on me without any notice was rude and an imposition. Like I said, you can stay a few days and go home. But my life doesn't revolve around you. I have to work, and because you wouldn't know it, tonight was the first real date I've had in years, and you interrupted it."

She scoffed. "You don't *date* other men, you screw them. You date *women,* and when this whole gay idea has been screwed out of your system, you'll settle down the way you should."

Bull shook his head slowly. "You're delusional, Mom," he told her in a whisper. "I like Zach, and I asked him out on a date because he's more than someone I want to mess around with. He's a kind, gentle person who's been through almost as much shit as I have. Only he can still smile and laugh—something I don't do very often anymore." Bull stood up. "So get your things. I'm going back out to talk to him, and when we're ready to go, we're leaving, and you can come or not. But you will be nice." His mother said nothing as she stood up and left the room. Bull followed her as far as the living room. Then he went out back and found Zach sitting in the swing. "I'm sorry."

"It's okay. She's your mother," Zach said softly. "I understand. You need to spend some time with her."

"She hasn't had anything to eat. But we'll stop after we take you home," Bull explained. Zach nodded, and Bull lightly touched his chin. "I don't want you to go. I'd rather spend the evening out here with you watching the sunset and waiting for the stars to come out." He leaned close and kissed Zach gently.

"It's okay. I really do understand. You should spend time with your mother. I'd give just about anything to be able to spend a little more time with mine." Zach's pain was clear on his face. "You should have the time you need with your mother."

"I'd rather be here with you," Bull said honestly and stood up. Zach did the same, and Bull kissed him again. Then he picked up the glasses and wine he'd never gotten a chance to open and carried them inside. He set the bottle and glasses on the table and returned to where Zach stood on the deck, looking out over his small yard. "I really am sorry."

"It's okay," Zach said with a smile. "I had a nice time."

"I did too," Bull said and leaned on the railing, his arm touching Zach's. "Do you think we could go out again? I'd like to have you over for dinner sometime. I don't get to cook very often, but I like it."

"You cook?" Zach asked. "I never would have guessed that."

"I bet there are lots of things about me you'd never guess."

Zach turned toward him. "I bet there are." The knowing look in Zach's eyes was both comforting and sent jitters through his stomach. Zach knew some of the things that Bull rarely talked about and he hadn't run away, but Bull couldn't help wondering how he'd react if he knew the rest. "I can't wait to find them out. You're a fascinating person, Bull."

He shook his head. "No, I'm not."

"You are to me," Zach said, moving closer. Bull pulled Zach into his arms, kissing him deeply. He felt so right in his embrace, their bodies pressed together. He ached inside his pants and felt reciprocating excitement from Zach. Bull moved his hips slightly, and Zach moaned softly into their kiss. For an instant, Bull thought about his mother and how she'd feel, but those thoughts didn't last long, not with Zach filling his ears with tiny whimpers that nearly had him coming in his pants.

Zach jumped as the door behind them slid open. His mother cleared her throat. Bull sighed and nipped lightly at Zach's lower lip before releasing him. Then he turned toward her. "I found this on the table, I hope it's all right," she said, raising her glass before taking a huge gulp of the wine. Bull clenched his fists. He'd bought that bottle especially for Zach and him to have on their date. It was a wine to be savored, for a special occasion, not be swilled and gulped like something from a box.

Bull growled and strode past her and into the house. He recorked the bottle and put it away. Granted, it wouldn't keep now that it was open, and he could get another bottle, but it pissed him off. "Let's go," Bull said as he motioned his mother inside. He managed a smile for Zach, because even though he was pissed as hell, it wasn't Zach's fault Bull's mother felt entitled to whatever she wanted. He and Zach followed, and Bull closed and locked the sliding door. When he turned around, he saw his mother upending her glass. She held the glass toward him like he was supposed to refill it. He took it instead and set it in the sink.

"Are we going to take the Mustang?" Zach asked quietly, and Bull shook his head, leading them to the Camry he drove every day.

Bull unlocked the car, and his mother leapt for the front door. Bull shook his head and got in as well, making sure Zach was situated before starting the car and pulling away. He pulled to the main street and prepared to turn toward Zach's apartment. "I'd like to eat there," his mother said, pointing across the way.

"Fine. We can stop on the way back," Bull said sharply.

"It's okay," Zach said from behind him, and Bull felt a soft pat on his shoulder. He switched the direction of his turn signal and made the left turn, then the immediate right into the restaurant parking lot.

Thankfully, they weren't busy, and the host showed them directly to a table. Bull placed Zach next to him and took his hand beneath the tablecloth. His mother asked for a glass of wine as soon as the waiter approached the table. "I'm sorry, ma'am, we don't serve alcohol. You're free to bring your own and we'll be glad to pour it for you," he said and then took their drink orders.

"I forgot how ridiculous Pennsylvania is about alcohol. Imagine a nice restaurant not serving wine," she said more loudly than was necessary, as though someone were going to hear her and instantly change the law just for her. Zach ordered a Diet Coke, and Bull did the same. They got an order of bruschetta to split while Bull's mother ordered a full meal.

"Have you been seeing my son long?" Bull's mother asked Zach.

"I met him at his club, and we had lunch last Saturday. Afterwards, a guy mugged me, and Bull came to the rescue," Zach said and then looked at him. "This is our first official date, I guess." He squeezed Bull's hand.

"So this is new," she said.

"Mother," Bull warned softly, but as deeply as he could. The server brought her dinner salad, and for a few moments she was quiet.

"You know I don't approve of... this...." She waved her fork at both of them.

"Bull is a good man," Zach interrupted, and Bull watched the full effect of his mother's steely gaze fall on Zach. "He's caring and thoughtful, although he doesn't want most people to know that. He's also more than capable of making his own decisions." Zach leaned over the table. "He has told you he's gay, right?" Bull's mother's eyes widened and she nodded. "So is it me you object to? Or that you won't accept facts?" Zach's voice was soft, but his words seemed to carry immense weight. "If you loved him, you'd accept Bull for who he is and not what you want him to be." Zach turned toward Bull. "I wish I'd had the chance to say that to my own family."

Bull nodded his understanding and turned to his mother, who looked completely shocked. "I want some wine," she said, obviously avoiding Zach's question. Instead, she drank her water. The server brought their appetizer to share, along with his mother's fish. She ate it in silence and kept reaching for a wine glass that wasn't there. To say the rest of the meal was strained was a vast understatement. Bull watched his mother eat silently. He and Zach talked quietly and ate their bruschetta. By the time they were done eating, Bull could have cut the tension with a knife. Zach had quietly apologized to him no less than six times, telling Bull he felt bad for imposing. "It's not your fault," Bull whispered more than once.

After a seemingly interminable amount of time, the server brought their check, and Bull placed enough bills in the folder to cover it along with a nice tip. "You don't need to leave that much," his mother said, reaching for the folder. Bull took it and placed it out of her reach before standing up. He waited for her to walk toward the door before following with Zach. He tried his best to ignore the way she was acting and enjoy being with Zach, but she was sucking any fun or liveliness out of the room.

Silence prevailed for the rest of the ride to Zach's apartment. Bull parked the car and walked Zach to his door.

"I had a wonderful time and—"

"You don't have to say it. She's your mother and she is the way she is. You can't change her any more than she can change you, thank God." Zach looked dramatically toward the starry sky. "I am sorry I opened my big mouth, but I meant what I said about you, whether she wants to hear it or not." Zach opened the door to the small entranceway, and Bull followed him inside and up to his apartment. He waited while Zach unlocked the door and then he followed Zach inside. Once Zach had closed the door, Bull pulled him into an embrace. "I don't think I'll ever get tired of holding you." He leaned down and kissed Zach hard.

His body reacted instantly, and while the last thing he wanted was to go out to face his mother with a hard-on, he wouldn't change the time he had with Zach for anything. Zach moaned softly and held on as they deepened the kiss. "I wish you could stay," Zach said breathlessly.

"Me too," Bull agreed. "But I'll call you soon, and we'll get together without my mother tagging along." God, that was so damned embarrassing. "Have a good day at work tomorrow, and I'll call you, I promise." Bull got one more sweet kiss and then turned to leave the apartment before he decided to let his mother sit in the car while he took Zach to his bedroom. His heart pounded and his breathing raced as he pulled open the door, said good-bye, and then descended the stairs. He sighed as he pushed open the outside door and walked to the car.

"Well, that was a mealtime experience I don't want to have again," his mother said as soon as Bull got in and closed the door.

Bull clenched the steering wheel as his frustration rose to the surface. "You chose the restaurant, you ordered the food, and you did everything in your power to make the conversation around the table as unpleasant as possible." Bull's jaw ached, he was gritting his teeth so hard. "I really wish I understood you, but I don't. There's no making you happy."

"Sure there is," she said pleasantly. "Find a nice girl and get married."

Bull snapped his head around to her. "Right," he scoffed, trying to keep from yelling at her. "Make some girl and myself unhappy so you can be happy. I don't think so. You just need to get it through your bleached head that I'm not going to do that. I've done things in my life I'm not proud of, but the people I hurt deserved it. Some innocent girl does not deserve to spend the rest of her life with a man who does not and will never love her."

"I thought the military would have worked all that crap out of you," she spat.

"The military taught me the meaning of honor and integrity, two things you know very little about." Bull's hands began to ache and he pulled them away from the steering wheel. His mother turned away and looked out the window. "You can be as high and mighty as you like, but I don't need someone to take care of me and I'm not the one who's gone through six husbands hoping to find one who'll put up with me for more than two years."

"You don't need anyone," she countered softly, and Bull knew she was close to tears. That was the one thing he could not stand, so he closed his mouth and started the engine. He backed out of the space and drove toward home. Neither he nor his mother said a single word. Bull pulled into the drive and up to the garage door. He turned off the engine. Closing his eyes, he waited to see if she'd say anything.

"I'm sorry I'm such an awful mother."

Bull rolled his eyes, but he didn't rise to the bait. "You'd be a lot more pleasant to have around if you listened and didn't act as though you were entitled to run my life." The implication hung in the air that she could barely run her own life, let alone anyone else's. He got out of the car and waited while she opened the door and got out. She was obviously hurt, but Bull was determined not to back

81

down. They'd had similar confrontations and conversations every time she visited. What never ceased to amaze Bull was the fact that his mother loved the boys at the club. She had no problem with gay people. What she didn't like was having a gay son.

"But I'm your mother," she said, falling back to her old standby.

"Yes, and I'm an adult, able to make my own decisions. So you need to make an effort to realize that at this point in my life, I don't need you. I'm grown and don't need my mother any longer. I haven't needed you in my life for a long time. Therefore, if you hope to have a place in my life at all, it's going to have to be because I *want* you to, not because I need you."

She whipped her head around toward him. "You don't mean that."

"Of course I do. Just because you're my mother doesn't guarantee you a place in my life."

"But you owe me," she said.

Bull squared his shoulders and stared her straight in the eyes. "I owe you nothing. After Dad died, you weren't around very much, let alone the mother I needed. Why do you think I left home and went into the service right after graduation? Oh, and while we're at it, why do you think I stayed away for almost three years? I took my leave and saw the world, but I rarely saw you." She faltered and reached for the car for support. "I'm sorry if this hurts you, but it's the truth. You haven't been there for me in any way in years. But I've done right by you. So now it's your turn. You need to make a choice about whether we have a relationship at all." Bull turned and walked away.

He reached the door to the house before his mother said a word. "Do you have any fond memories of me?" she asked.

"Yes," Bull said and pulled open the door. "They're from a long time ago, but there were way too many walks home from school because you forgot to pick me up or coming home to find you passed out drunk on the sofa. And let's not forget the parade of stepfathers."

His mother swallowed. "They weren't all bad," she said.

"No, they weren't. But the good ones figured you out eventually and left. The others hung around until you left them. So maybe if you want to be treated better and cared about, you should start with the person in the mirror." Bull held the door and waited for her to walk inside. He closed and locked the door behind them and walked silently to the kitchen. He poured his single evening scotch and sat in his chair, ice tinkling as he slowly sipped from the glass. When she joined him, Bull got up and poured her half a glass of white wine before putting the bottle away. Then he sat back down and closed his eyes, ignoring the silent tension in the room. "I still miss Dad," he confessed.

"Me too," his mother said. "Every single day." He watched her tip back the glass and then pause before taking a sip instead. "More than anything I want him back."

Bull finished his scotch and set the empty glass on the small table next to him. "I'm the only part of Dad there is." He'd been thinking a lot about that lately. "I've spent the past sixteen years trying to figure out why he had to die, and I've spent fourteen of those years hating you for trying to forget him. The stepdads knew what you were doing—at least, Roger did. He told me after you split up. He was the best of them all—a good, kind man. I wasn't able to see it then, but I can now." Bull shifted in his chair. "I still talk to him. He calls or I call every few months just to talk."

"Does he ask about me?"

"No. That's the agreement. We don't talk about you because you broke his heart. I think he really loved you, and I think it hurt when he figured out he was just a substitute." Bull stood up, deciding it was time to go to bed. He'd had enough emotion and drama to last him for months. "He's getting married again in a few months, and he asked me to the wedding." Bull stepped over to his mother and took the empty glass she was cradling in her hands. "Go on to bed. You've got to be tired." He lightly touched her shoulder and then took the glass into the kitchen.

"Where is he getting married?"

"The wedding is in North Carolina," Bull explained. He didn't tell her that he'd not only been invited, but Roger had shocked him and said he wanted Bull to be his best man. Or more accurately, he'd said he'd wanted his son to act as best man. Bull thought about that conversation as he walked down the small hallway to his bedroom. That day on the phone had been the first time he'd cried over anything since his father had died. And there was no way he would tell a living soul. "In late August," he added. Roger and Bull's mother had divorced about eight years ago now, and Bull was pleased to see Roger move on with his life. "Are you going to bed?"

She nodded and got up from the chair. Bull paused and waited until she was in the guest room before checking all the doors and turning out the lights. Then he went to his room and got undressed and ready for bed. His head spun with all the surprises and theatrics of the past few hours. Life was so much easier when all he had to do was look menacing. People stayed out of his way, behaved, and there were no messy emotional complications.

As soon as he turned out the light and closed his eyes, the single reason why he was pleased things didn't always work out that way flashed through his mind. Bull smiled as he thought about Zach and how amazing he'd felt in his arms. On the days he didn't work, Bull always had trouble falling to sleep. He knew he should simply stay up until three and then try to go to bed. That was what he normally did. But his mother was in bed, and if he rambled around the house, he'd only keep her awake. At nearly midnight, he called Harry, who told him everything was fine. The club was having a normal Thursday night, busier than the other weekday nights, but nothing like Friday and Saturday. "Everything is fine, there's no need to worry," Harry told him. "How did your date go?" The beat of the music wafted in from behind Harry.

"It was fine until my mother showed up," Bull explained.

"Ouch," Harry told him. "Wait, you didn't say your mother was coming."

"I didn't know. She drove up from Florida without telling me," Bull whispered. "Zach and I were sitting in the backyard, getting to know one another, about to open a bottle of wine, when there she was in all her disapproving glory." Bull ran his hand over his head and down his face. "She was rude to Zach and insistent as hell. We ended up taking her somewhere so she could eat, and then I took Zach home."

"Let me guess: after you left Zach, you and your mom had one hell of a fight," Harry said.

"You can quit with the grin I know you're sporting right now. And yeah, we had a fight of sorts. I did most of the talking. I don't know if it did any good, but she was quite subdued when she went to bed." Bull listened for any sounds in the house, but everything outside his room was quiet.

"That must have made you feel better." Harry had heard a lot of Bull's stories about his mother, and he'd fielded more than his fair share of Bull's grumpiness after he'd spoken with her.

"It really didn't," Bull said. "I always thought letting her have it would feel good. But it was just sad. She's my mother, and neither of us gives enough of a crap about the other to care how we feel. She appeared on my doorstep, full of her usual self-importance and entitlement. I let her have it because...."

"Jesus," Harry said, and this time Bull knew he was grinning. "That's the most you've talked about your feelings in four years. Say, would you put the real Bull on the line? I want to talk to him."

"Smartass," Bull muttered.

"Thank God. I was beginning to wonder if something had happened to you." Harry chuckled. "Go on to bed and don't concern yourself with anything here. I'll see you tomorrow night, and don't worry about your mother. They're all a pain, but you only get one. So talk to her in the morning and see if you can't work the shit out between you. And try not to growl too many times while you're at it." Harry laughed and disconnected the call.

Bull placed the phone on the nightstand and then turned off the light. He stared up into the darkness, wondering what he was going to do about his mother. Those thoughts fell away fairly quickly, and he drifted off to sleep thinking of Zach.

THE NEXT two days were a jumble of logistics: trying to get his mother where she wanted to go, despite her having her own car; working; and then attempting to get enough sleep. He couldn't help notice the two fresh wine bottles in the trash each night when he got home. Hopefully he would be able to get his mother on her way home in the next day or so. It was well after noon on Sunday when his phone woke him up. He searched for it without opening his eyes and nearly knocked it onto the floor. "Hello."

"Gosh," Zach said. "I figured it was late enough that I wouldn't wake you."

"It's okay," Bull said as he cracked his eyes open and glanced at the clock. He yawned. "I should be getting up. My mother has had the run of the house for hours, and Lord knows what I'm going to find." He sat up and let the covers pool on his lap. "I'm glad you called." He'd been wondering if he and his mother had managed to scare Zach away.

"I wasn't sure how busy you'd be with your mother there." Zach sounded nervous. "She didn't like me."

"It wasn't you. My mother's delusional sometimes." Bull stretched his legs and thought about getting up and dressed, but he was too damned comfortable, and listening to Zach's voice had certain parts of him very awake. Bull slid his hand under the sheet and along his shaft. "Like I said, I'm glad you called." And getting happier by the moment.

"I didn't know if you might want to have lunch or something," Zach said a little nervously. "Just you and me," he added, and Bull chuckled.

"I would. Mom is supposed to be spending the afternoon with some old friends." Bull pulled his hand away from his dick when he heard sounds in the other part of the house. "I could pick you up in an hour, if you like."

"Yeah, that would work," Zach agreed. "I'll see you then." They ended the call, and Bull got out of bed, stretching his back and neck. He thought about taking a shower, but that would only lead to him using the soap to relieve the pressure, and Bull really hoped that after they had lunch, dessert would be offered. He shaved and cleaned up before dressing and padding out to see what his mother was up to.

She met him in the living room, and his eyes widened when he saw her. "You look very nice." Her simple dark-blue dress highlighted her eyes.

"I'm hoping a change to the outside will help with the inside," she explained and picked up her purse from the sofa. "Darlene and I are planning to have dinner, so I'll be back later this evening." She seemed energetic and actually smiled.

"Are you okay?" Bull asked.

"Never better. I had some time to think, and I realized I was turning into my mother." Her smile slipped from her face. "While you were at work, I didn't have much to do, so I looked around and saw the picture you have hanging in the hallway. I thought it was an old picture of me at first, and then I realized it was Mother. I look just like her. Then it hit me that I was acting like her too. She was bitter and obnoxious after Daddy died. I must have latched on to that and run with it." She reached out and stroked his cheek. Bull almost stepped away. He couldn't remember the last time she'd touched him with tenderness. "You were right the other day. I avoided my mom after I got married because she was miserable to be around." His mother sighed. "I can't say I can change overnight, but I'm going to try to be more pleasant."

"Okay," Bull said.

His mother checked her watch and then headed for the door. "I'll see you tonight. Have fun," she said and left the house.

Bull stared after her, wondering what in hell had just happened. Maybe his mother had been visited by the ghosts of mothers from hell—past, present, and future. Bull didn't move for a while, shocked into inaction until his stomach rumbled and he remembered his appointment with Zach. Then he sprang into action and got ready to leave. He drove to Zach's and parked outside his building. Zach must have been watching, because he bounded out of the brick building and down the walk to Bull's car.

"I figured you'd be hungry," Zach said as he slid into the passenger seat.

"I am," Bull said and leaned over to Zach. Food could wait. He tugged him into a kiss that quickly heated. The seats crunched softly as they moved closer to each other. When they separated, Zach was flushed and his breathing shallow. He sat back in the seat, and Bull glanced down and noticed the tent in his pants. Zach shifted and turned away slightly, and Bull knew he'd been caught looking. Not that he cared, but Zach blushed even harder. "Let's get some lunch."

Zach opened his mouth to say something but ended up just nodding. Bull drove to a brewpub that had great burgers and made the best beer in town. Once they were seated and the server had provided them with water while they looked over the beer menu, Zach began the conversation. "So, how was your mother's visit so far?"

Bull shrugged. He wasn't ready to count today's behavior as a permanent change. Not yet.

"Your mother's quite…. It was interesting to meet her, and…." Zach swallowed. "She seemed…." He was obviously searching for something nice to say and kept coming up short.

"There are times when my mother puts the bitch in obituary," Bull said, and Zach howled, snorting water out of his nose. Bull reached for some napkins and helped him clean up the mess. "I heard that once from one of the drag queens and I thought it appropriate in this case. Are you okay?"

Zach nodded, gasped, and looked like he was still trying to contain his laughter. "Warn a guy next time, will ya?" he said, wiping his face and then turning away to blow his nose. Then he turned back and began to laugh again. Their server took their drink orders, and after they both requested a beer, the server carded Zach and then hurried away.

"I wish they'd stop carding me," Zach said as he put his license away.

"Consider it a compliment. No one has carded me in years," Bull told him.

"No one would dare," Zach said and fell into a fit of giggles. Bull glared at him. "Come on, you're huge, bald, and obviously no kid." Zach took a gulp of his beer. "I, on the other hand, look about twelve."

"No, you don't," Bull whispered deeply and saw Zach shiver. "You're...." Bull searched for the right word. The ones he usually used to describe guys didn't seem to fit. Not that Zach wasn't hot and sexy, because he was. But those terms seemed too shallow. Zach was much more than that. "Perfect," slipped past his lips.

Zach scoffed and rolled his eyes. "I certainly am not."

"See, that's why you're perfect. You're attractive but don't stand around waiting for everyone to look at you. You're sweet and kind, but not sugary. That's what makes you so wonderful." God, he was actually gushing a little. He never gushed. He turned away and growled at himself so he'd feel better.

"I'm just me," Zach said. "If you want to talk hot, then you should look in a mirror." Zach tried to cover his blush with his glass but it didn't work. Bull saw it and smiled.

"You don't have to be embarrassed," Bull said. That blush was way too cute.

Their server returned and they ordered lunch. Once the server left, Zach seemed more comfortable. "How is everything going at work?" Zach asked.

"It's the same. People are getting sneakier, and Saturday night I caught one of the bartenders trying to let someone into the back door of the club. At first I figured it was just a friend, so I watched the guy, but then I kicked his ass out when I saw him dealing. Then I fired the bartender."

"How did you know who let the guy in?"

"Cameras," Bull said. "I installed a tiny one in the back that activates when the door is opened. Most of the time the camera films the guys taking out the trash. Didn't take us long to figure it out, though. How's work for you?"

"Same as always. I have made progress with the comic book, though. I think it's going to be really cool," Zach said. "I'll show it to you once I have the story all laid out. Then you can tell me what you think."

"I still can't believe you turned me into a comic book hero," Bull said, unable to suppress a smile. He'd been smiling a lot more in the past week.

"Why not? You inspired me," Zach said.

The server brought their lunches, and they both dug in. Zach was obviously hungry, because he ate almost as ravenously as Bull. They talked a little, but mostly they chowed down. Bull had observed one very basic difference between men and women. As a kid, he'd gone out with his mother and her friends a few times. The ladies would order and talk, eating their food over a full hour. Not any of the guys he knew. When you put food in front of them, their heads lowered, and conversation generally ceased or descended to short questions with even shorter answers.

"I didn't realize how hungry I was," Zach told Bull after they'd both nearly cleaned their plates.

"I was starving. Last night was busy as hell, and I didn't get a chance to grab any sort of snack. Once I got home, I was too tired to cook."

Their server stopped by the table and asked if they'd like another beer. Bull declined because he had to drive. He knew he could safely have another, but he didn't want to risk it. They both switched to soda and finished their lunches.

Zach sat back in the chair, his eyes half-closed, patting his belly. "Dang, I'm full," he said. "I don't think I'll be able to eat a thing for at least two hours." He grinned. "My mother always said I was part hummingbird because I eat all the time and run it off."

"I can see that," Bull said. "I used to be that way, but I'm not as active now, so I watch what I eat. Without a lot of intense activity, I can really pack on the weight." He patted his belly and noticed Zach's gaze following the movement of his hand. Their server returned and asked if they wanted dessert. When they both declined, he left the check. Zach reached for it and opened his wallet. "I can get that," Bull said.

"It's my turn," Zach said with a slight challenge as he pulled out the cash.

"At least let me leave the tip," Bull said. He knew Zach was trying to make ends meet and didn't have a lot of extra money. Zach agreed, and Bull pulled out some cash and placed it with Zach's. He still appeared uncomfortable. "What is it?"

"Do you see me as the girl?" Zach asked.

Bull was taken aback for a moment. "No. I don't date girls. Never have. Well, not since high school, and then they were only friends. There's nothing wrong with treating the person you're dating with care and respect."

Zach nodded slowly. "Do you always... go out with guys like me?"

"Are you asking me if you're my type?" Bull questioned.

"I guess so," Zach said.

Bull sighed. This was a difficult question for him, because he'd never really given it much thought. "Usually the guys I take home look more like me. They're big and tend to be tough looking. I think mostly because they're the ones who have the courage to actually approach me. Most guys don't." Bull gazed into Zach's eyes, registering his confusion. "You never seemed afraid of me." Bull paused, afraid he wasn't making sense. "To answer your question, yes, you're my type, if only because you had the courage to look past my intimidating exterior," Bull said in what he hoped was a playful way.

Zach must have understood because he giggled slightly. "You hide behind that tough façade, don't you?" Bull didn't answer. That question hit a little too close to home. "I guess we all hide certain parts of ourselves in different ways."

"Yeah, I guess we do," Bull agreed. The server took the folder with the check and money, and they got up from the table. "Would you like to come back to my house? My mother is out and won't be back until sometime this evening." Damn, that sounded way too high school for someone in his thirties. "What I mean is, we'll have some privacy." Bull was a huge fan of privacy right now.

"That would be nice," Zach agreed, and they left the restaurant. Unfortunately, the initially sunny morning had darkened, with thick clouds building in the west.

"I'd hoped we could sit outside, but I don't think that will happen," Bull said.

As they approached the car, the hair on the back of Bull's neck stood straight up.

"Is something wrong?" Zach asked, picking up on his reaction.

"I feel like we're being watched," Bull said. He walked around to his side of the car and unlocked the door, using the shift in angle to peer around them. Movement at the far side of the parking lot caught his attention. He opened the door and waited for Zach to get inside.

"What's going on?"

"I'm not sure," Bull said as he started the engine and backed out of the parking space. He paid close attention to the other cars he could see. "Did you notice someone watching us while we were in the restaurant? Someone who might have been trying to blend in, but was doing something out of the ordinary?"

"Like a guy ordering food, but not eating it?" Zach asked.

"Exactly," Bull said, checking his mirror once again but knowing he wouldn't see anything. "What did he look like?"

"Not as tall as you, with really dark hair, cut short. He wasn't really big, but strong-looking." Zach looked around. "Oh, there was a tattoo of something on his arm, but…."

"It's okay," Bull said. He had a pretty good idea who it was. What he really needed to know was what in hell he wanted. He slowed down and drove more normally. There would be no tail because the man had no need for one. "You did a great job. Why'd he catch your attention?"

"He looked like someone who would make a great character for my comic," Zach said.

"I'll be sure to tell him that when we see him," Bull said. "His name's Spook—at least that's the name I know him by." He really should have spotted Spook earlier. He hadn't realized he was getting soft.

"If he's a friend, why didn't he stop by the table?" Zach asked.

"He isn't exactly a friend, more of an associate from my former life," Bull answered. "I doubt we're in any danger, because if he'd wanted to hurt us, we'd already know it." He reached over and patted Zach's leg. "I know him only by reputation, and he won't show himself again until he's ready."

"But what does he want?" Zach asked.

"I don't know," Bull fibbed. He didn't know the details, but he had a pretty good idea what Spook wanted and what his answer would be. But he'd cross that bridge when he came to it. He was sure Spook meant them no harm, and that was all that mattered for now. "But we're both fine." Bull squeezed Zach's leg again, enjoying the way his leg bounced with pent-up excitement. "Are you up for a glass of wine? If not, I have some beer," Bull offered as he made the turn down his street and parked just outside his garage. He hadn't seen anyone or anything unusual, but Spook was aptly named and would remain nearly invisible until he was ready to talk.

The first drops of rain hit the windshield as soon as Bull opened his car door—big, fat drops that made both him and Zach hurry toward the door to escape them. Once Bull had the back door open and they'd stepped inside, the sky opened up and sheets of water fell from the sky. Bull led them into the living room, and Zach sat on the sofa. Thunder rumbled around the house as Bull got them something to drink. He'd just returned and set down the glasses on the coffee table when a crack split the air. Zach threw his arms around Bull's neck and tried to climb him as the house shook and the lights went out.

"I take it you don't like storms," Bull said calmly as he sat down on the sofa. Not that he minded in the least.

"Hate them. Always have," Zach whispered, clutching Bull tighter as another clap of thunder rent the air. Zach shook in Bull's arms. Bull slowly rubbed Zach's back, and Zach closed his eyes, trying to calm as the storm raged on outside. As soon as the thunder dissipated, replaced by rain pelting the roof, Zach loosened his grip around Bull's neck. He tried to move away, but Bull held him in place.

"I like you like this," Bull whispered and then leaned in. The kiss began gently but quickly deepened and intensified. Zach whimpered softly, and Bull settled him on the sofa, cupping his cheeks in his hands and taking charge of the kiss. What surprised him was the way Zach kissed back, battling him for control. He liked it. Few of the guys he'd been with had been fighters. With his size, the guys who approached him were usually submissives who wanted Bull to take charge. It seemed Zach wasn't like those other men. He should have known, because Zach was so different from anyone he'd been with before.

Deciding to press his luck, Bull tugged Zach's shirt out of his pants and slipped his hands underneath, stroking Zach's silky smooth skin. Damn, he felt amazing—warm and sexy. Zach faltered when Bull stroked up his back. Bull shifted on the sofa, maneuvering Zach until he was on his back. Then he pushed Zach's shirt up his trembling belly before licking and kissing his skin. Zach gasped loudly and vibrated as Bull got his first taste. Bull was instantly addicted, and he pushed Zach's shirt up higher, then licked a small pink nipple. Zach groaned and shook beneath him.

"Bull," Zach said between panting breaths.

"Just tasting," Bull said and then captured Zach's pink lips in a near-bruising kiss that left them both breathless. He wanted to taste a hell of a lot more, but he wasn't sure if Zach was ready. Once they broke their kiss, Bull tugged off Zach's shirt and dropped it to the floor. Zach squirmed slightly, like he was trying to hide. "What? You're very handsome," Bull told him with a smile, but he saw a touch of fear in Zach's eyes. He backed away, and Zach stood to retrieve his shirt. "What happened?" Bull asked when he saw the marks on Zach's lower back.

Zach whirled around and held his shirt in front of him. "Parts of my family felt very strongly that sparing the rod spoiled the child."

"Your uncle?" Bull asked between clenched teeth. Zach nodded, and Bull saw red. "If he comes around here again, he'll find out how it feels to have someone whip him. I know people who are very good at it." He realized he was shaking and took a deep breath to try to calm himself. Then he reached out and tugged Zach to him. "Don't be ashamed. You didn't do anything wrong. Your uncle did." Bull kissed him again, and Zach hugged him, dropping his shirt.

"He did that when he found out I was gay," Zach whispered.

Bull held him tighter. He knew it must have hurt like hell, in more ways than one, to have been the subject of that kind of blind hatred. "What about your parents? Didn't they stop him?" Bull asked, afraid of the answer.

"They didn't know. While he was hitting me, he made it very clear that I was to get the hell out, not be seen, and if I told my parents what happened, he'd make sure they felt some pain as well." Zach was near tears. "I can see now that he's deranged and drunk with power, but at the time I was so naïve." Zach wiped his eyes. "I got accepted to college, and as soon as I had a place to go, I left."

Bull released him and tugged off his own shirt before pulling Zach close once again—this time skin to skin. Zach wriggled in his embrace, rubbing against him like a cat. "You have nothing to be ashamed of as far as I'm concerned. Wear those scars like a badge of honor; you earned them. You took the worst of what the old bastard had to offer and came out whole on the other side."

"No, I didn't," Zach said. "I came out scared of my own shadow, living in a strange place with people I didn't know. I went to class, did my homework, and hid myself away as best I could."

"But you're not hiding now," Bull said.

"No, I'm not," Zach told him. "And I don't want to talk about my uncle anymore." He smiled. "I think we can think of more pleasant things to talk about. Either that or you got me half naked for nothing." Zach chuckled, and Bull sat stunned. How on earth could Zach be so pleasant after telling him what had happened?

"Don't you ever get angry?" Bull asked. "You tell me about this stuff that happened to you and then act like it doesn't matter. I've had plenty of shit happen to me, and sometimes it's all I can think about." He could hardly believe he was telling Zach this. He never talked about feelings and shit with anyone. It was a sign of weakness. Doubt, fear, worry—you pushed them all down deep and forgot about them to get the job done. That was what he'd been taught in the service, and Bull had always been a good study when it came to that portion of his life.

"I guess I figured I could either laugh or cry," Zach explained. "No one wanted to be around me when I was angry and sad all the time, so I did my best to let it go. It didn't always work, but I've accepted what happened. My uncle can't hurt me anymore, and my parents are gone, so he can't hurt them either." Zach shrugged. "In a way, I'm free, so why would I want to be miserable?"

Bull shook his head and kissed Zach. "I think you might be the bravest person I've ever met."

"Yeah, right," Zach said playfully.

"I mean it. The men I was in the service with, the ones who could stare down death day after day, would rather die than talk about what they're feeling at any given moment. Hell, if someone hurt me like that, I'd wait for my revenge and then tear them limb from limb and make sure no one ever found the body."

Zach stared at him. "Sometimes you scare me."

"I don't mean to. All I'm saying is I'd take a much more physical approach to the problem, and then once it was over, I'd bury it away and never talk about it again."

"I'm starting to see a recurring theme here," Zach told him. "But, you know, it's okay to talk about stuff. I told you what happened, and you listened. You didn't judge me or think I was a bad person or that I somehow deserved what I got. You understood, or tried to. So why wouldn't you expect the same treatment from others?"

"Because it doesn't happen," Bull told him and then kissed Zach hard. It was time for this emotional, heart-to-heart stuff to end. So he figured the best way to do that was to distract Zach, and Bull knew exactly how. Zach stood in front of him, and Bull maneuvered him between his legs. They kissed, and then Bull gently sucked down Zach's neck, then continued across his chest before lightly sucking one of his pink nipples. Bull felt Zach's legs begin to shake with what he hoped was excitement.

"Bull," Zach said, thrusting his hips slightly forward. Bull smiled when he saw the obvious tent in Zach's pants, and he slowly opened Zach's belt, and then the catch on his trousers before letting them fall to the floor. "What are you doing?" Bull paused. "I mean, I know what you're doing, but—" Zach gasped, and Bull grinned before stroking him through the fabric of his briefs. "Is it supposed to feel like this?"

"How does it feel?" Bull asked.

"Like my head is going to explode, and I'm not going to be able to stop myself if you keep that up," Zach whimpered through clenched teeth. "I mean, I know what this is supposed to feel like, I have done stuff before, but it's happening so fast, and you feel so good, and…." Zach swallowed. "I like what you're doing, but am I going too fast?" Zach continued his shallow breathing as Bull slowly pulled down the front of his underwear until Zach's cock bounced forward. Bull stroked him gently, and Zach's words quickly turned to groans and whimpers.

Zach kept trying to catch his breath, but every time he seemed to, Bull took great delight in stroking him faster or gripping his long cock tighter. Within seconds, Zach went quiet and his head lolled back. Bull tightened his grip as Zach began pushing his hips forward. "That's it. Just give it up and let yourself go," Bull whispered. Zach's mouth fell open and he whimpered softly before stiffening as he came all over Bull's hand. Zach shook and continued whimpering, his eyes squeezed shut.

Once Zach had finished coming, Bull waited for him to come down from the endorphin high. "Wow," Zach said softly.

"I think I can agree with that," Bull said. He picked up his shirt and used it to wipe his hand, then tugged Zach down into a kiss. "Let's go to the bedroom," he whispered. Zach nodded and pulled up his pants from around his ankles. Bull took Zach's hand and led him down the hall to his room, then closed the door behind them. When he turned around, Zach stood by the side of the bed, holding his pants up. He looked adorably hot, and Bull couldn't help smiling.

Zach kicked off his shoes and then dropped his pants. He stepped out of them and stood naked except for his socks. Then he tilted his head to the side, obviously waiting for him. Zach was gorgeous, and Bull's mouth went dry. Zach wasn't particularly tall, but slim with a flat belly and chest. He wasn't a gym bunny, but who cared? His smooth skin glowed, and when Zach turned to the side to move his clothes out of the way, the profile of a dimpled butt came into view. "Beautiful," Bull whispered, the only word that came to mind.

Zach looked down at himself. "Are you just saying that?" Bull growled. "Okay," Zach held up his hands and smiled. "You never just say anything."

"Damn straight," Bull stated without taking his eyes off Zach. He toed off his shoes and then pulled off his belt. The buckle hit the floor with a soft ting that neither of them paid much attention to. "And to answer your earlier question, you are most definitely my type." Bull's cock had throbbed in his pants for the last half hour, and Bull sighed as he opened his jeans and popped the buttons on his fly. Zach's eyes widened as Bull stepped out of them and tossed the pants aside, his boxers tented prodigiously. Then Bull slowly stepped toward Zach. He could see the excitement, tinged with worry, in his eyes.

"I've never...." Zach swallowed.

"We're not going to do anything you're not ready for," Bull soothed and reached to the nightstand for a bottle of lube. He placed it on top and closed the drawer. "All I want you to do is what makes you happy." Bull took Zach into his arms, holding him close and slowly rubbing his back. When they kissed this time, it felt like electricity ripping through him. "Do you feel that too?" Bull asked, his lips right next to Zach's.

"Yeah," he whispered. "Is that zing normal?"

"It's never happened to me before," Bull said, slightly confused.

"That must mean I'm someone special," Zach said. He slid his hands down Bull's back and into his boxers. Bull started slightly when Zach cupped his butt. He never let guys do that to him because it might give them ideas, but he wanted Zach to touch him and he didn't care where.

"Sweetheart, I knew you were someone special the first night I frisked you and you giggled and wriggled right there on the sidewalk." Bull kissed Zach again, and Zach pushed Bull's boxers down until they slid on their own down his legs. Bull stepped out of them and then pressed Zach onto the bed. Their lips barely parted as Bull maneuvered Zach up until his head rested on one of the pillows. Then, once he knew Zach was comfortable, all bets were off. The only problem was that he couldn't find a position that wouldn't press all his weight onto Zach. That little dilemma was settled as Zach squirmed from beneath him and pressed Bull onto his back before nearly jumping on top of him.

"Dang, you're...," Zach began, but Bull kissed the words away. Their bodies fit together well despite their differences in height. Zach vibrated on top of him, his long cock sliding beside

99

Bull's. The sensation made Bull's eyes roll back into his head more than once. Then Zach pulled his lips away, and Bull opened his mouth to protest. "I want to see you," Zach said, and then he shifted until he sat across Bull's legs.

Bull puffed out his chest, and Zach chuckled. Zach stroked his belly and up across his pecs before lightly tweaking Bull's nipples. "I knew you would be hot. I could tell that from the way your black T-shirts always looked two seconds from ripping, but I guess I expected you to have a tattoo or something."

"I nearly got one when I was in the service," Bull admitted, stopping when Zach wrapped his fingers around his thick cock and began stroking. "Jesus, you want me to talk while you're doing that?"

"I could stop," Zach said, pausing the glorious movement. Bull growled. "Okay, then," Zach said and resumed his movements. Bull had been touched plenty in his life by himself, and by other guys. But no one had ever made him feel like this, not even Junior, his first... really his *only*... lover.

Bull sat up, reached for Zach, and tugged him down and onto him. They kissed hard, and Bull cupped Zach's butt, then pressed their hips firmly together. Zach thrust slowly, and Bull did the same, rubbing and stroking while they kissed each other nearly to oblivion. The intense heat from Zach's body wrapped around Bull like a comforting blanket that he never wanted to crawl out from under. Zach filled the room with small moans and whimpers that quickly worked their way into Bull's heart.

He rolled them on the bed after a few minutes. Zach groaned with mild frustration, and Bull chuckled slightly before kissing his way down Zach's neck and throat before licking long wet trails over his hot skin. Huge bursts of rich musk and a slight sweetness tingled against Bull's tongue. He licked and sucked Zach's nipples, accompanied by moans that increased in intensity the more he sucked. "Bull," Zach whined.

Bull smiled, then kissed and licked down Zach's chest and belly to where his cock bounced and throbbed against his belly. Bull

100

opened his mouth and sucked in the head of Zach's cock. He jumped slightly, and Bull peered up to make sure everything was okay.

"Jesus!"

Bull sucked Zach deeper as a steady stream of awed moans and whimpers filled the room. "Has anyone ever done this before?" Bull asked. Zach rolled his head back and forth on the pillow. "Then are you in for a treat." Bull sucked Zach deep, letting his flavor burst on his tongue. For a few seconds, Bull thought Zach was about to scream, but he settled into steady groans and whimpers. Soon Zach was moving slightly along with him, lifting his hips off the bed.

Zach was getting close—Bull could tell by his breathing and the intensity of his moans. He pulled away, and Zach sat up, eyes wide open, probably wondering what was going on. Bull kissed him and settled on the bed next to Zach, holding him close. Zach returned his kisses and then pressed him back on the mattress before settling between Bull's tree-trunk legs. Zach stared at him for a few seconds, and Bull sat up and lightly stroked over Zach's shoulders. "You don't have to do anything you aren't ready for," Bull whispered.

"It isn't that," Zach said. "What if I'm not any good?"

Bull chuckled. "With lips like those, you'll be a natural." He brought a finger to Zach's lips and lightly traced over them. "You kiss like a dream. So don't worry about things like that. Simply be yourself and do what makes you happy and what you think I'll like."

Zach kissed him and then slowly licked down his chest. Bull settled back on the mattress and let Zach find his way. He groaned at the warm pleasure that spread through him when Zach licked a nipple. He hissed when he sucked and then bit lightly, because it felt so damned good.

"Where'd you learn to do that?"

"I might not have much real world experience, but we nerds do read... a lot," Zach told him.

"Those must be some good books," Bull said, and Zach hummed his agreement as he licked and sucked a trail down Bull's hairy belly. He seemed fascinated and lightly ran his fingers over Bull's chest and stomach.

"You're really sexy," Zach crooned. "I like hairy men."

"Then we both get what we like." Bull moaned when Zach gripped his cock, stroking lightly as he shifted.

Bull watched, fascinated as Zach slid his pink tongue along his length. Bull clamped his eyes closed without even thinking about it, reveling in the gentle sensation. Bull reminded himself he'd promised Zach he could explore on his own. Normally about this time, Bull would take charge and go for what he wanted. He gripped the bedding and held still, willing Zach to suck him. Bull sighed and groaned when he felt Zach's lips slide over the head of his dick. Zach went too fast and quickly backed away.

"Take your time and don't go too deep at first. That takes practice," Bull coached, and Zach took him again.

The wet heat that surrounded him nearly took Bull's breath away. Zach wasn't polished or practiced, but damn if he wasn't enthusiastic. He used his hand, lips, and tongue all at the same time.

"I like that I can make you do that," Zach said, stopping for a second to breathe.

"What?" Bull asked.

"Make those whiny sounds," Zach said. Bull would have growled, but Zach sucked him again and the thought zipped from his brain. All he wanted was Zach's lips and hands on him. Everything else was immaterial, including whatever sounds he happened to be making. Bull clutched the bedding as his body reacted. It wasn't long before he neared the edge. Bull cupped Zach's cheeks and lightly tugged him upward until their lips met. Bull reached for the lube and squirted a little on his hand. Then he worked his hand between them and coated both their cocks. Zach sighed and began pumping his hips, rocking slowly against him.

"That's it," Bull said encouragingly, stroking down Zach's back and cupping his butt. He then thrust upward. Within seconds they were moving together, the bed rocking with them.

Zach held his breath, and Bull could tell he was close. He was quickly approaching the edge as well. Zach groaned and stiffened. Bull thrust hard, desperate for the last bit of sensation that sent him plummeting into his release. Zach followed right behind, both of them filling the room with their cries.

Bull closed his eyes and floated, keeping his arms around Zach, carrying him along on his quiet, euphoric fantasy. He didn't want to move, and Zach seemed content to stay where he was too. So they lay there holding each other.

"Is this okay?" Zach asked after a while. "I'm not too heavy?"

"You're perfect," Bull said lazily. He didn't even have the energy it would take to open his eyes.

"Do you have to go to work?"

"No," Bull whispered.

"Good," Zach said as he rested his head on his shoulder. Neither of them made any effort to separate. "Did you ever have a boyfriend?"

"Once," Bull said, "a while ago. His name was Junior."

"Where is he now?" Zach asked, lifting his head and meeting Bull's gaze.

"He's dead," Bull answered, and Zach lowered his head back to his shoulder.

"Is that why you're so closed off sometimes?" Zach asked. Bull had been lazily rubbing Zach's back. He stilled his hand.

"Maybe. I don't know. Things between Junior and me were rocky—sometimes really good, other times not so much. Things ended badly, and then they ended for him permanently." Bull sighed. He didn't want to talk about this. "We don't have to talk about everything, do we?"

Zach lifted himself up. "No." He continued shifting away from him. "You know, I heard the rumors that all you wanted were guys to take home to fuck," he told Bull and got off the bed. "I guess I was pretty stupid to think I might be different. That you saw me as something more." Zach hurried around the room, gathering his clothes. "All that nice talk and everything else was just a huge pile of shit to get me to sleep with you, wasn't it?"

"No," Bull said. "It certainly was not. If that was all I wanted, I could get that any night." As soon as the words were out of his mouth, he wished he'd kept his big mouth shut.

"Yeah, you probably could. So was I some challenge?" Zach began pulling on his clothes.

Bull climbed off the bed and walked to where Zach was working to yank on his shirt. "It wasn't like that at all. I care for you, and you are much more than just sex. But there are things that are hard for me to talk about." At least that made Zach pause. "To answer your question, yes, I think Junior is the reason I keep away from everyone. You can't get hurt if no one gets close."

"And you always guarantee you end up alone," Zach added. Bull knew he was right, but he wasn't ready to talk about what had happened. Too many things had all gotten wound together for him to just open up.

"Give me some time," Bull asked and reached out to Zach before gently pulling him into his arms, although honestly he wasn't sure which of them was in real need of comforting. "I haven't thought about all these things in a long time. I need a chance to process it."

"How can you not think about it? Do you have some superpower that allows you to forget the stuff you want to? Because, man, I'd like to be able to do that. I could forget about what my uncle did to me and what happened to my parents. I could wipe away the fact that everyone I grew up with hates me because of who I am." Zach trembled, and Bull held him tighter. "I'd really like to forget that part," Zach whispered against his neck.

"It doesn't work like that. But you learn to suppress things, and I've kept a lot of stuff locked away for a long time," Bull said. He was really good at it. All the mental military training came in very handy. Whatever he didn't like or couldn't deal with, he simply pushed aside and never thought or talked about again. At first it was difficult, but after a while it got easier and easier, though he'd gotten grouchier and pulled away from more and more of the people in his life. "Goddammit!"

"What?" Zach asked.

"My mother was right." Damn, he hated when that happened. Bull led Zach to the bathroom, where they cleaned up the remnants from earlier, and then they went back to the bedroom. They climbed on the bed, and Bull held Zach while staring at the ceiling, wondering just what he'd unlock if he opened that huge box of crap he'd been carrying.

CHAPTER
SIX

ZACH HAD no idea what to think. He'd talked to Bull a few times over the past few days, but he was having a hard time with the way Bull kept everything closed off and bottled up inside. "I want to be in a relationship with someone I trust," he told his buddies as he set a bowl of chips on the coffee table.

"Sometimes it takes time. Trust doesn't happen overnight, and for some people trust has to be earned," Jeremy said as he reached for a handful of chips and then began popping them into his mouth one at a time.

"I just don't know." Zach flopped onto the sofa and grabbed his sketchpad from the coffee table before something got spilled on it. He'd made a lot of progress on his comic and the story seemed to be coming along well. He'd decided that when his hero was in bull form, he wouldn't be able to speak. He could only grunt and growl the way Bull seemed to when he was angry or trying to avoid a subject. Kevin took the pad and began looking through it. "Did I tell you about this guy Bull called Spook, who was watching us when we went to lunch?" Zach said. "Bull said he was someone from his past. Then he said this Spook guy was nothing for us to worry about because if he'd wanted to hurt us we'd already have known it. I mean, what else is going to show up? I already met his mother. She makes Jane Fonda in *Monster-in-Law* look like Julie Andrews."

Kevin closed the sketchpad and whapped him on the head with it. "Doesn't matter what you say, we know the truth. Every time you talk about the big lug, you go all gooey-eyed. You care for him and you're sitting here worried about him."

"I just wish he'd talk to me," Zach said. After what they'd done, he was feeling a little insecure, because no matter what Bull said, Zach was still afraid he was just a lay and nothing more.

"Give him time. This is the kind of guy who doesn't wear his heart on his sleeve. He has secrets and he's done things that he can't talk about." Jeremy munched on another chip and turned back to the television. "You said he was a mercenary, and to get the job done those guys sometimes have to do things that aren't necessarily aboveboard."

"Yeah," Zach said, leaning back on the cushion. "I just wish he'd tell me instead of hiding stuff."

Kevin snorted, as did Tristan. "You have things you don't want to talk about. So does he, and he's older than you, so he has more years of dumb stuff to not talk about. Give the guy a break," Kevin told him. "Bull obviously likes you. He actually talks to you without grunting, growling, or telling you to get the hell out of the line."

"Did it ever occur to you that he might have reasons for not wanting you to know?" Tristan asked, and everyone turned to him. "Maybe there are dangerous things in his past. He actually said there was nothing to worry about because if this Spook guy wanted to hurt you guys, you'd already know it. That sounds pretty ominous to me. I mean, this is Harrisburg, not some hotbed of spy-versus-spy stuff, and yet he's got a guy watching him who could kill him?" Tristan shifted closer to the edge of his seat. "If you want my advice, I'd say ignorance is bliss, and I sure as hell hope none of Bull's friends—or worse, enemies—are following me around." Tristan reached for the bowl of chips and then stopped. "Have you seen anyone else following you or had the feeling you were being watched?"

"No," Zach said, but Tristan had a good point, and his nerves went through the roof. "But I probably wouldn't know unless they decided to confront me or something." God, what if they tried to kidnap him or hurt him to get at Bull? Would Bull even care? Zach shivered and slumped into the sofa cushions.

"Okay, that's enough," Kevin told Tristan. "All you're doing is scaring Zach." Tristan and Kevin had a mini glare-fest for a few seconds, and then Kevin turned to him. "On a brighter note, did you notice that Brantley wasn't in the office today?"

Zach smiled slightly. He'd had a great day at work. The tension usually present in the office seemed, if not gone, at least less intense. "I thought he was on vacation or something," Zach said.

"He is. A permanent one. It seems a list of the crap he'd been pulling managed to filter its way to the president's office." Kevin grinned and tilted his head to the side modestly.

"You didn't," Zach said, and Kevin shrugged. "How?"

"Let's just say it looks like some anonymous person saved a bunch of documentation, dumped it into an envelope, and when they were in New York, dropped it into the mail." Kevin could barely sit still. "He was pulling so much junk that could get him in trouble, it wasn't even funny."

Zach took a deep breath and then released it. That was one huge complication in his life that had been removed.

"Is there any more beer?" Jeremy asked as he added his bottle to the small collection of empties on the coffee table.

"No, those were the last of them," Zach said. He'd thought he had another case. "There's a beer distributor just around the corner. I can get some more." Zach stood up and started heading to the door.

"It isn't really necessary," Jeremy said.

"Come on, guys," Kevin encouraged. "We're celebrating the demise of one of the world's great assholes. We have to have one more beer so we can toast our freedom."

"I'll go with you," Jeremy offered, and he followed Zach out of the apartment and down to the sidewalk. "So," Jeremy began as they walked. "You really like this guy, don't you?"

"Yeah," Zach admitted with a smile. "He's, like, hard as rock on the outside, but melty chocolate on the inside. He growls a lot and looks tough, but he's always nice and kind to me. I don't know why he shows that side of himself to me sometimes, but he does, and I keep thinking that's a big leap for him."

"Are you sure about all this?" Jeremy asked. "Not that I want to put a damper on your happiness or anything, because you're a good friend, and you've been happier these past few weeks. It's good to see. You weren't sour or anything before, but you have a spark you didn't have before." Jeremy nudged his side. "Or is that because you're getting laid?"

"Maybe a combination of both," Zach offered wickedly and then broke down into laughter. "The sex was nice, but…."

"You want something more?" Jeremy asked. "You sound like a girl."

"I do not. My folks loved each other and cared for each other and me. I know yours divorced, but I saw how happy my mom and dad were when they were together. It didn't matter how bad things got, because they had each other. I guess I want that same thing." Zach glanced at Jeremy as they walked. "Maybe I should just sow my wild oats and screw everything that moves, but I don't want a revolving door on my bedroom."

"Does Bull want the same thing? See, that's the trick: both people wanting the same thing at the same time, and maybe he doesn't," Jeremy said as they approached the corner. "He is older than you…."

"Yeah, so he should be ready to settle down," Zach said. "After all, I already met his mother and survived it. You'd think that since I didn't go running for the hills I'd be a definite keeper."

Jeremy chuckled slightly. "Maybe he'll never want to settle down. Have you thought of that? Or maybe he wants someone his own age." Zach growled, and Jeremy giggled. "Did you pick that up from him?" Zach growled again and held his serious expression for about two seconds, then smiled. He knew what Jeremy said was a possibility, but one he didn't want to fathom. He really liked Bull, and he thought Bull liked him. He hoped Bull *more* than liked him, but he wasn't going to go too far down that route.

They approached the beer store, and Zach held the door open for Jeremy. "This is such a pain," Jeremy mumbled as they walked inside. The alcohol purchase system in Pennsylvania was bizarre to say the least. Wine and liquor had to be purchased at the state stores, six-packs of beer could only be purchased in bars, and beer by the case was only sold at beer distributors. "The whole system sucks," Jeremy continued as they wandered down the aisles stacked with cases of beer.

"I know," Zach said as he trailed behind. They had this same conversation whenever they were together and alcohol shopping was on the agenda. They found what they wanted, and Zach lifted the case of Miller Lite to carry it to the registers. "Jeremy," he whispered, and motioned him over from where he'd been looking at the Sam Adams none of them could afford. "That's the guy," he said, turning toward the back of the aisle as Spook rounded the end of the aisle.

"Are you sure?" Jeremy asked. "What's he doing here? Do you think the business is a front for something?"

"What should I do?" As soon as the question crossed his lips, he knew Jeremy was going to be no help. Zach pulled his phone out of his pocket and tapped in Bull's number as he left the aisle, moving in the opposite direction of the other man. "Bull," Zach whispered when his call was answered.

"Are you okay?" Bull asked.

"I'm at the beer store near my apartment, and that Spook guy from the restaurant is here. What should I do?" Zach's entire body shook with excitement.

"Nothing. Leave him alone and let him leave," Bull said. "No, wait.... Walk up to him and tell him Bull wants to talk to him now. Then pay for your stuff and leave. That ought to shake him up enough that he'll contact me."

"Okay," Zach said, his heart thumping. "Should I tell him to meet you at the club?"

"That won't be necessary. He'll already know how to get in touch with me." Bull paused. "I want you to call me when you get home."

"I will, and you need to call me later," Zach said, and Bull promised he would. Zach hung up and walked through the store and up to the counter. He set the case down and told the clerk he'd be just a minute. Jeremy stayed by the counter, and Zach wandered back down the other aisle and up to the smaller man. For a second he wasn't sure, but then he saw the tattoo. With his heart pounding, he walked up to the man. "Bull said he wants to talk to you."

Spook whipped his head around to him and his mouth dropped open for a second before he said, "You're the guy from the restaurant—"

"Bull wants to talk to you, Spook," Zach interrupted and then turned and walked back up to the counter. He paid for the beer, then he and Jeremy left the store and walked briskly back toward the apartment. No cars followed them and no one tried to stop or talk to them. His phone rang when they were a little more than halfway home. Zach handed the beer to Jeremy and answered the call.

"Where are you?" Bull asked.

"Jeremy and I are on our way home. No one is following us or anything. That Spook guy was sure shocked. He recognized me from the restaurant, but I caught him by complete surprise."

"Okay." Bull sounded nervous. "Go home and stay there." He swore under his breath. "Having you approach him was probably the dumbest thing I've ever done. Make sure there are people around, and I'll be there as soon as I can. Promise me," Bull added before Zach could say anything.

"Okay, we're almost there. The guys and I are watching movies and stuff, so we'll keep the door locked and wait for you," Zach said. He started walking faster, his heart racing.

"Good. I'm already on my way to my car," Bull said. Zach hung up but kept his phone in his hand. They entered the building and climbed the stairs, then let themselves into the apartment. The other two guys barely looked up from the television. Zach closed and locked the door behind them. Then he placed some beer in the refrigerator to chill and filled a pan with ice for the rest. He sat with them to wait, ignoring the television while Jeremy told the others what had happened at the store. Once Jeremy was done, the guys peppered Zach with questions he couldn't answer and went instantly silent when a brisk knock sounded on the door.

"Is that him?" Jeremy asked. Zach checked the peephole and unlocked the door. Before he could say anything, Bull surged inside, closed the door, and engulfed him in his strong arms.

"Are you okay?" Bull whispered into his ear. "Telling you to do that was the stupidest thing I have ever done in my life." Bull squeezed him and Zach held him back. "I should have had you just go home."

"Umm, guys," Tristan said from behind him. Zach groaned because he didn't want this to stop.

"Bull," Zach said, and he released him, but stood close. "These are my friends—Jeremy, Tristan, and Kevin. They were with me at the club." Bull nodded to all three but didn't say anything.

"Maybe we should be leaving," Tristan said, but none of them made any sort of move. Bull growled and they all stood up.

"Do you think it's safe?" Kevin whispered.

"It should be fine," Bull told them, and they all grabbed their things and filed out.

"You certainly know how to clear a room," Zach said.

"They're safest if they're at home," Bull told him and then started wandering around the apartment. "Go on and pack a bag. I don't want to leave you alone."

"Why not stay here?" Zach asked.

"Because that bed is way too small for the both of us, and I intend to keep you extremely close," Bull told him. Zach swallowed. "I know you probably think I'm overreacting, and maybe I am, but…."

"Just say it," Zach said as he pulled out his bag and put a few things in it.

112

"I was scared half to death as soon as I hung up the phone," Bull admitted, and Zach figured that was as close to a declaration of Bull's feelings as he was going to get. Zach finished packing his things and turned around. Nervous energy radiated off him.

"Is there something you aren't telling me?" Zach asked.

"No. I...." Bull paused. "I was just... concerned." The nerves seemed to slip away, replaced by the in-charge guy Zach was used to seeing.

"Because you care or because you felt responsible?" Zach asked. He set the bag on the bed and crossed his arms over his chest.

"Fuck," Bull said.

"Maybe, but only if you answer my question," Zach pressed. This was fun. A small vein on Bull's forehead throbbed.

"You're a...," Bull started. "Because I care, all right? I was worried because I care about you, and as soon as you hung up I went crazy worrying I might have put you in harm's way."

Zach moved closer. "Was that really so hard? I care about you too." He reached up and threaded his arms around Bull's neck. "There's nothing weak about telling someone they mean something to you."

"There is if they use it against you," Bull corrected, and Zach gasped.

"Did this Junior person you mentioned do that?" Zach tightened his arms. Bull didn't answer, but he didn't need to. Zach could already see the answer in the swirl of conflict in Bull's eyes. "If he wasn't already dead, I'd kill him."

"Okay, tiger," Bull said, pulling him close. "Let's not get all wound up. Have you got your stuff for work?"

"Yes. I just need my sketchbook and then we can go." No way would he leave that behind. If everything worked out, he hoped he would get a chance to draw Bull a few times. Zach rested his head on Bull's chest. "I'm glad you came over. I missed you." They shared another hug, and then Zach got his things. As he was leaving, he remembered the beer sitting in ice in the sink. He ran back and took care of that before he locked the door and followed Bull out to his car.

THE MAN drove like a bat out of hell, weaving around cars on the road and racing through traffic signals. Zach held on the entire way and kept quiet, hoping they arrived in one piece. At the house, Bull parked in the driveway and got out of the car. Zach waited while Bull checked the backyard and then around the house before unlocking the door and walking inside.

The man Zach had seen in the beer store sat at Bull's kitchen table.

"I got your message that you wanted to speak to me," Spook said evenly, watching Zach the entire time. "I guess I thought you'd be alone." He got up from the table and walked toward the door. "Maybe another time."

"No, you'll talk now, or leave and not come back," Bull growled.

"Not in front of him," Spook said. "He's not part of this."

"You made him part of it when you did such a sloppy job watching us at the restaurant," Bull said in a low, threatening tone. "Just so we're clear, since we've never actually met, I'm Bull, and I know you're Spook. Your reputation precedes you, although I'm a little surprised Zach, here, was able to make you at the restaurant." Bull put his arm protectively around Zach, and Zach moved closer. "I hadn't noticed you until I caught a glance of you in the parking lot, but Zach saw that you'd ordered but weren't eating." Spook's gaze shifted to him, and Zach thought he saw a touch of respectful surprise. "So do you want to tell me what you were contracted to tell me?"

Spook sat back down at the table, but said nothing. "The client is very secretive, and we have specific instructions to speak only to you."

"Then you can tell the client my answer is no and be on your way. I've been out of the business for the past four years, and I'm not particularly interested in taking any new jobs. I have a good life and I don't want to take a step backwards into the life," Bull answered forcefully.

Spook met Bull's gaze. "You know it's never that easy. This particular client has an affinity for your work, and he doesn't take no for an answer." Zach looked from Spook to Bull and instantly knew that Bull knew who Spook was talking about. "He also has a very long reach and a very delicate job that needs to be done."

Zach swallowed hard and waited for Bull's response. "Tell the client," Bull began slowly, "that I will not be bullied and that things have changed. I have not been in his employ for some time. I always keep my word, but if threatened, certain information will find its way to people your client will not be pleased about. Some of this information could prove lethal for your client." Bull remained calm, but Zach was getting more and more nervous. He tried to follow this conversation, but too many details had been left out.

"That would be a violation of all agreements," Spook said.

"True, but your client forgets that death severs all agreements, and I have engineered things so that my continued health will ensure your client's continued health and prosperity. However, his own government would not be pleased and would find itself quite embarrassed by the information I have. He knows the action his government has taken and would take under those circumstances." Zach saw no tension in Bull's expression. "So, as I said before, tell your client no. I'm retired and wish to remain that way. He needs to find someone else to clean up his messes." Bull went silent. Spook stood up and walked around them to the door without saying another word.

"I'll relay the message," Spook said. Zach looked at Bull and then back at the door. Spook was already gone.

"What the hell was that?" Zach asked a little more loudly than he intended.

"That's how you turn down an offer you can't refuse," Bull said. "The man making the offer is very powerful. World-level powerful."

"Then how can you turn him down?" Zach asked. "Not that I want you to go anywhere, but this is scary. What if he hurts you?" He slowly moved closer to Bull. "I don't want anything to happen to you."

"I have some material on the man making the offer that will give him pause. But this is only the opening salvo," Bull said. "Spook's client won't take no for an answer. He'll simply try to find another way to make his offer." Bull pulled out one of the chairs and sat at the table.

"You're okay with this? How can you be?" Zach asked. "He wants to take you away. I'm not dumb. If you accept this thing, then you'll be gone for a long time." Zach's mouth went dry.

"I have no intention of going anywhere. Like I said, he won't take no for an answer, but in the end he'll figure out he has to," Bull said. "I have no intention of working for him. Hell, or seeing him ever again." Bull's gaze became as hard as steel. "I'm just saying that sometimes it takes more than once before someone who's very used to getting his own way accepts a refusal." Bull tugged him close. "I don't want to do those kinds of jobs any longer."

"Were they bad? Did you do bad things?" Zach asked and then wished he hadn't. "Sorry, I shouldn't have asked."

"No, I've given it some thought and I should tell you at least part of it. I was a mercenary, hired to protect and perform tasks in foreign countries where our government couldn't or wouldn't go. Anyway, the man who wants me to work for him is one of the worst, and I had the misfortune of saving his life once. I should have let the bastard die, but hindsight is always perfect. Anyway, I didn't assassinate people, if that's what you're thinking, but I did fight the causes of the people who hired me, and that meant killing people on the other side." Bull stammered slightly. "In the service, I was good; after I got out, I was better. I honed my skills and gained a

116

reputation for being able to get into very tight situations and out again without anyone knowing."

"Okay, I don't really understand," Zach said. He was trying, but Bull was still speaking cryptically.

"It doesn't matter. I don't want you stained with that history. Anyway, it was in one of those situations that I saved this particular man's life, as well as the life of his son."

"Junior?" Zach asked, and Bull nodded.

"He and I became friends and then something more. His father is from a country and culture where two men together are not tolerated. Junior and I made plans to leave and return to this country together. See, I thought he loved me. We were together almost a year. He and I did jobs together, and at the end of the last one, he came to the US with me as a student. His father arranged for him to go to college here. We could be together in this country, where it was safe." Bull swallowed hard. "Somehow his father found out, and while his father didn't condemn either of us, he would not condone the relationship either. Eventually, Junior left and returned to his father's family, but not before he blamed everything on me. I had led him astray, and now Junior had seen the light and wanted to return to his family."

"He turned on you after all you'd done for him?"

"Yup. Junior returned to his family, and I went my own way. Our paths didn't cross for almost two years. By then, Junior's father had forgiven both him and me. I was requested on another job by Junior's father, and Junior asked to go along. Neither his father nor I thought it was a good idea, but Junior was insistent."

"Did he make your life miserable?" Zach asked, trying to imagine what it must have been like to work with someone who'd betrayed him like that. Zach knew he'd probably have kicked him in the nuts or something.

"No. We were supposed to clear out a group of nomads from an area that Junior's father wanted to develop. Junior worked with me and the team to develop a strategy to get the job done with as little bloodshed as possible."

117

"Did you become lovers again?"

Bull nodded. "He told me he'd been wrong earlier and that he should never have left. I can still see his long, black hair, and his deep-as-night eyes tearing up as he asked for forgiveness." Bull choked up. Zach was afraid to move in case Bull stopped, but after a few seconds, he moved closer to comfort him. "We spent the days working and our nights together for almost a week." Bull sniffed once and then stared at him. It seemed somewhat shocking to see the strong and confident man Zach had come to know reduced nearly to tears. "It turned out the nomads were more than we were led to believe, and they had the firepower of a small army hidden among them. When we tried to move them on, they opened fire. It wasn't pretty, and a number on both sides died." Bull took a deep breath. "After it was over, I found Junior—his real name was Khalil—on the ground. At first I thought he was only stunned, because I saw no injuries, but his eyes were open and set. He was already dead, shot in the back multiple times. The team cleaned up the situation, and I carried Junior's body back with us and made sure he made it to his family. I mourned him alone and kept our renewed relationship a secret from everyone. Telling his family would have hurt them and tainted his memory, so I did what my military training had taught me and shoved all of it into a tiny box. His father mourned a son he was proud of, and I quietly mourned a lover that I could never acknowledge again. That was my last job. I went back to the States, turned down every job offer I got, and managed to renew my friendship with Harry. Eventually we opened the club together. And I haven't heard from Junior's father again until today."

"I'm sorry," Zach whispered.

"I know. It's hard to talk about. See, he left me the first time, but he promised me that once that job was over for his father, he would come back to the States with me. He wanted a life that didn't include lies."

"Did you believe him?" Zach asked.

"Yeah, I did. He showed me a plane ticket and said he wanted to be with me. The next day he was gone. I spent years trying to forget him, and then I had him again, but he was taken away. After that, I decided it wasn't worth it."

"That's where you were wrong. Because it is worth it," Zach told him. "Am I worth it?"

Bull stared at him. "How'd you get to be so smart?"

"I'm not. I know what I want, though." Zach moved closer, stroked Bull's cheek and ran his hand over his forehead and across his smooth, shaved head. "Don't ask me why, because you can be the most exasperating man I have ever met, but I want you. There's something about you that gets my blood racing and my heart pounding. When you kiss me, I can barely breathe, and when I look at you, my mouth goes dry." Zach touched Bull's chin until he raised his gaze to meet Zach's. "If this is some casual thing, then you need to tell me now. If this was just a quick roll in the hay, I can deal with that. But I cannot deal with being on the receiving end of what Junior did to you. I can't and I won't. I deserve better than that, just like you deserved better than that from Junior." Zach stared hard at Bull.

"This isn't casual," Bull said. "I don't know what it is exactly, but I…."

"Small steps. As long as you're willing to be honest, I can handle it," Zach said. He knew that opening Bull's heart would take patience, but deep down he thought it would be worth it. Zach leaned forward, touching Bull's lips with his own. Bull wrapped his arms around him, tightened his hug, and deepened the kiss. Within seconds, Bull was kissing him hard, taking possession of Zach's mouth. The kiss became almost bruising, but there was no way he wanted it to stop. Bull needed reassurance, and Zach sure as hell intended to give it to him. "Why don't you lock up, and I'll be waiting for you in your bedroom."

"Okay," Bull answered. Zach backed away and watched Bull leave the room. He loved to watch him move, every muscle pressing against the fabric of his clothes. It was truly a sight to behold. Then Zach walked out of the kitchen and down the hall, where he pushed open the door to Bull's room with its king-size bed. He pulled down

119

the covers and positioned the pillows before stepping out of his shoes. Then he stripped, climbed onto the bed, and rested his head on one of the pillows, lightly stroking his cock so everything would be good and ready when Bull came in the room.

Zach heard a small gasp. He turned his head and saw Bull standing in the doorway. "Damn, that's beautiful." Zach blushed. "You lie there naked, your dick hard and sliding through your hand, and when I tell you it's a beautiful sight, you turn red." Bull stepped into the room, and Zach watched, completely enthralled, as he began pulling off his clothes. Bull's wide shoulders and muscled chest came into view when Bull opened the buttons of his shirt, then shrugged it off and tossed it over the chair. Bull opened his pants and then turned around and pushed them down his legs.

"And you thought I was beautiful," Zach whispered in reference to Bull's beefy butt. He shifted onto his knees and reached out, stroking it through the fabric of Bull's boxers. Bull looked over his shoulder and shoved his pants lower before turning around and moving slowly toward the bed, his thick, heavy cock swaying rhythmically.

Bull placed his hand in the center of Zach's chest and pressed him down onto his back. Zach held his breath and waited excitedly for what Bull had planned. "Close your eyes," Bull whispered, but Zach hesitated, very much wanting to see everything. Bull stilled completely and stared at him. Zach knew nothing would happen until he complied, so he slid his eyes closed and waited.

Bull's hot, wet tongue swirled around a nipple, and Zach gasped and tried his best to hold still. He wanted to see Bull lick him, but he did as he was told and kept his eyes closed even as Bull did things that made his skin tingle and his breath hitch over and over again. Bull sucked and licked at both nipples until Zach's mouth hung open. He gasped for breath and only seemed able to make moaning and whimpering sounds that became more and more desperate as the seconds ticked by. His cock throbbed and pulsed against his belly. Zach reached for it, but Bull gently batted his hand away. "Just be patient," he whispered. "This is all about heightening the fun."

"But you'll kill me first," Zach whispered.

"No, I won't, and I promise you'll thank me," Bull told him. Then he kissed him hard before saying, "Keep your eyes closed." Bull licked down Zach's neck and throat before sucking his nipples and then licking his chest and stomach. Zach's muscles rippled as he felt Bull's tongue. He gasped when heat beyond belief slowly slid up his cock. It had to be Bull's lips. He moaned loudly and clamped his eyes closed tighter, gripping the bedding as Bull sucked his cock.

"Bull, that's not fair," he mumbled blindly. "I want to see you."

"For now just relax and enjoy," Bull whispered and then sucked him deep and hard. Zach's head came off the pillow and he gasped, tearing at the bedding as he tried to control his body. Already it was betraying him, tingling and throbbing as he tried not to come so quickly. His feet throbbed and his legs vibrated as his balls pulled up toward his body. He was seconds from coming when Bull backed off and let him slip from his lips.

Zach opened his eyes, and Bull stared back at him. "I never was good at following directions."

Bull smiled and moved closer, resting part of his weight on him, pressing Zach into the mattress. Zach wrapped his arms around Bull's neck and held on as they kissed, chest to chest, hips to hips, rubbing their cocks against each other. Zach closed his eyes once more as the intensity of the sensation built.

"You are so beautiful," Bull said.

"Isn't that from a song?"

"Yes, but I won't sing it, I promise," Bull said before kissing him again. "Now I'm going to taste you until your head explodes and you can't remember your name." Bull slid down his body and sucked him hard, sliding up and down his cock until Zach could barely see. His entire body vibrated with excitement as ecstasy quickly built. Within a few minutes, Zach could no longer control his body. Bull sucked his cock, bobbing his head until Zach's toes curled. The pressure built and built until he gave in completely, clutched the bedding, and let go.

He came so intensely he saw stars and shook the entire bed. It took him a few seconds before he realized the screams that reached his ears were his own. Then he slumped back on the bed, trying to breathe while he floated on clouds of happiness. Nothing mattered, and on the periphery of his consciousness he was aware of Bull moving around him. Then he felt warm arms encircle him, pulling him close. Bull lightly stroked his belly as Zach came back to himself. Then Zach slowly opened his eyes and curled his lips into a smile. "Jesus," he whispered.

"I know," Bull told him. "Do you have any idea how hotly adorable you look when you come? Your eyes glaze over and your mouth hangs open." Bull lightly stroked his lips. "I could watch you in the throes of passion for the rest of my life."

Zach opened his mouth to respond, but stopped himself.

"Just relax," Bull said.

"What about you?" Zach asked.

"That was just to take your edge off," Bull told him and nuzzled his neck. "I intend to take you right back there as soon as you have a chance to catch your breath."

"You *are* trying to kill me," Zach said, cradling Bull's head. "What a way to go." He lay still and let the remnants of afterglow settle over him. There was plenty of time; they had all night, he hoped. "What about work?"

"Don't you worry about anything," Bull said. "I already called Harry and things are covered. It was more important that I make sure you were safe."

Zach hummed his agreement. "Do you think Spook will be back tonight?"

"I doubt it," Bull said. "But I want you safe with me just to be sure. I wouldn't put it past some people in my former profession to use whatever leverage they could find to get someone to do what they want. And right now, to me, and to them as well, you would be leverage, because I would do a great many things to see that you were safe." Bull sighed, then lightly touched Zach's chin and turned his head. He kissed him so gently yet intensely that Zach felt it in his heart. Bull had just told him he cared. In his own way, Zach realized Bull was letting him know what he meant to him. Somehow Zach doubted Bull was likely to say the three magic words, but his actions spoke volumes, and Zach was content. Bull was a man of action, not words.

"I know what it took for you to tell me what you did tonight. And I know what it meant. I trust you too," Zach said, cupping Bull's cheeks in his hands and guiding their lips together. "I think I'm ready for what you promised." Zach smiled and then kissed Bull hard.

Bull took over from there, and for the next half hour, Zach was kissed and licked to within an inch of his life. The things Bull did to him and the places he touched blew Zach's mind. When Bull sucked him deep and slipped a finger inside his body, Zach thought his head would explode. But that was only the beginning. One finger became two and then three. Zach tried to form words, but none came. He could only manage groans and whimpers. When Bull lifted his legs, placed his feet on his shoulders, and rolled on a condom, Zach thought he'd die of anticipation. And when Bull pressed into his body, he tensed and thought the sensation would short-circuit his brain.

"Relax," Bull whispered. Zach tried, and the initial pain melted into pleasure as his body adjusted to the intrusion. Within minutes, Bull was deep inside him, and Zach felt connected to another human being in a way he'd never thought possible. Then Bull began to move, and Zach wondered if he'd ever get enough oxygen into his lungs again.

Zach locked gazes with Bull, and Bull leaned forward, capturing Zach's lips in a deep kiss. The world seemed to stop, and then, once Bull broke their kiss, Zach watched as he straightened up and began rolling his hips. Bull touched something deep inside him, and Zach's eyes rolled into the back of his head. Zach had never seen anything sexier in his life, and he'd never felt so high and so amazingly special in his life. "I always thought I was a freak, different from everyone else," Zach whispered and then lost track of his thoughts when Bull slowed his movements, dragging his cock across the spot deep inside. Zach gasped and vibrated with years of pent-up passion.

"You're no freak," Bull said between gritted teeth, pressing deep and then holding still. "But, honey, you certainly are different." Bull leaned forward and wrapped his arms around him. Zach shifted his legs and circled them around Bull's waist. Then Bull lifted him, still buried inside, and pulled him to the edge of the bed. Bull stood on the floor with Zach on his back on the mattress. "You're an angel, and I want to take you to heaven." Bull withdrew, holding still just inside his body, and then slowly filled him again.

Zach moaned long and low, losing control. He was Bull's and he wanted it that way. His head throbbed and he tried desperately to catch his breath, but there was no way. "Bull," Zach whispered. "I...." He swallowed the words as Bull drove deep inside him.

Zach reached out, barely able to reach Bull's chest. With his fingertips he stroked Bull's heated chest, his soft hair tickling lightly. Bull leaned slightly closer, and Zach continued caressing his chest, desperately needing to be in contact with Bull in as many ways as possible. Once he had what he wanted, Zach clenched his muscles, and Bull gasped.

"Damn, sweetheart," Bull said with the sexiest growl ever. He picked up speed, and the bed shook with every thrust. Sweat beaded on Zach's skin, and Bull's body glistened.

Then Zach felt Bull falter. They gasped together. Bull took his hand off one of Zach's hips and wrapped his fingers around Zach's cock. He stroked to the time of his thrusting, and Zach pushed his hips upward to meet each thrust. As soon as he did, he nearly screamed with unabashed delight. He had no idea what to do. Everything brought more pleasure, more sensation, and he was on the cusp of completely overwhelming passion. "Bull, I'm all yours. Take me," Zach whimpered. He was on the verge of tears and had no idea why. Bull gripped him tighter, stroking faster.

The tingling started at the base of his balls and quickly spread through his entire body. Bull moved faster and faster, thrusting his chest forward as his lungs filled with air. Time stopped for Zach, and all that existed was Bull and the amazing way he was playing his body.

Zach clamped his eyes closed, gritting his teeth as pressure built higher and higher, until he could no longer contain it and came with a long shout of joy that went on and on. Then everything stopped.

"Zach, sweetheart," Bull said, stroking his cheek. He opened his eyes and saw Bull's eyes, filled with concern. "Are you okay?"

"What happened?" Zach asked, taking quick stock of himself.

"You passed out," Bull told him, "and managed to scare me to death."

"Wow," Zach said, afraid to move. His head throbbed, but other than that he felt amazing. His skin tingled and he was as relaxed and happy as he could ever remember being. "Did you...?"

"Oh yeah," Bull whispered and slowly pulled out. Zach lowered his legs, but didn't move otherwise. Everything felt too good to spoil. "Come on," Bull said and guided him back up until his head rested on a pillow. "I'll be right back." Bull walked to the bathroom, Zach watching his butt as he moved.

"What's that smile for?" Bull asked as he walked to the bed with a cloth.

"You," Zach whispered, trying to make his throat work. "You make me happy."

Bull stopped midwipe. "I don't think I've ever made anyone truly happy before." Zach placed his hand on top of Bull's. "I don't really know if I ever made Junior happy. I'd like to think I did, but I was never sure."

Zach took the cloth and wiped his skin before setting it aside. Then he took Bull's hand in his. "I want you to think of the last night the two of you were together. Did he look at you the way I am now?" Zach paused. "Did his eyes glaze over, and even in the darkness, you knew he was looking at you?" Bull nodded slowly. "Then you made him happy," Zach said with a lump in his throat. Bull leaped forward, encircling Zach in his arms.

Zach held him too, and Bull rested his head on his shoulder. There was no sound other than Bull's breath in his ear for the longest time.

"Thank you," Bull whispered.

Zach's heart warmed. He had never been in love before, but he was sure this was it. He held Bull tighter as the realization washed over him. He was in love. He closed his eyes and let the happiness wash over him. He knew this wasn't going to last. Something would happen—it always seemed to. But for now, in the quiet of Bull's bedroom with him in his arms, he'd enjoy it and take it for what it was.

"Let's go to bed," Bull whispered.

Zach reached over and turned out the light, plunging them in darkness. Bull shifted on the mattress and then pulled him close. Zach was pretty sure Bull loved him in return. He only wished he knew for sure.

CHAPTER
SEVEN

BULL HANDED the kid's ID back to him, growling, and motioned him out of line.

"What the hell did you do that for?" Harry whispered from behind him. "Let the kid in and have one of the guys man the door." The anger in Harry's voice caught Bull's attention. He motioned to one of the bouncers, who took his place. Bull went inside and threaded his way across the dance floor before making his way to the office. "I'm your oldest friend," Harry said and then shut the door. "Now tell me what the fuck is wrong with you! For the past week, ever since you took that last-minute day off because Zach needed your help, you've been impossible to be around and a complete asshole to everyone. Did Zach dump you? Because if you've been acting like this around him, I wouldn't blame him. Half the people in this club would dump you three times if they could."

"Rashad wants to hire me," Bull answered flatly. "And he isn't taking no for an answer."

"Is that what Spook wanted?" Harry was the one and only person Bull confided in. The two of them had very few secrets, and the great thing about Harry was that he knew how to keep one. Never had he breathed a word of anything Bull told him, and Bull carried Harry's secrets behind an equally tightly locked compartment in his head. He'd sooner die than betray Harry's trust.

Bull explained to Harry about seeing Spook. "Yeah. He delivered a message of potential employment, and since then he's talked to me twice, each time trying to feel me out to see what it would take to get me to do this particular job. I know it's hard to break out of the life, but I've been gone for four years and I don't want to be hauled back in. Not now."

"Does Rashad know about you and Junior getting back together before he died?" Harry asked.

"God, I hope not. He was angry enough the first time." A thought occurred to Bull. "Maybe he does know and this is how he's decided to deal with me."

"If he wanted to kill you, I suspect he'd find an easier way." Harry shook his head. "Junior's gone and nothing will bring him back, not for him and not for you. You didn't kill him and aren't responsible for his death, and you did everything in your power to protect Junior's family, even to your own detriment."

"It doesn't matter. I led the mission. We should have planned more, done more recon...," Bull protested.

"I can't understand what you went through or what that life was like, but I can tell you this: shit happens. As for Rashad, keep telling him no if that's your answer, and stop making everyone else's life miserable. I'm here for you if you need me." Harry clapped him on the shoulder. "Now quit being an asshole."

"Thanks. I know I can always count on you," Bull said.

"You bet you can. Who else would actually dare to tell you when you're acting like an ass?" Harry pulled open the office door and left, with Bull following right behind.

Bull went back to work, on edge like he hadn't been in months, watching everyone in the club for anything out of the ordinary. He saw the usual bad behavior and put a stop to it, but right now, he was looking for anyone who might be watching him. He saw no one, but that didn't mean they weren't here, only that he hadn't spotted them.

"Hi, Bull," Zach said, interrupting his thoughts.

"What are you doing here?" Bull asked, more forcefully than he intended, and Zach's smile diminished.

"I came to see you," Zach answered. "You've been avoiding me all week, and I was beginning to wonder if I'd done something wrong."

"I haven't been avoiding you." He had, but not in the way Zach meant.

"You've been talking to that guy Spook, haven't you?" Zach asked quietly, and Bull nodded while he focused his attention on the room. It was hard, because all he wanted to do was look at Zach and imagine what they'd do when they were alone. "Have you decided to take that job and haven't told me?"

"No," Bull said. "I haven't taken the job. I've been staying away so you'd stay off their radar and out of their line of sight." Zach was his weakness. He'd come to realize that during his near-panicked trip to Zach's apartment after he'd given Zach that stupid advice. If they really wanted him to do something, all they needed to do was put pressure on him through Zach, and Bull would do just about anything to keep him safe. Bull was falling in love. He knew that, and it scared the hell out of him. He kept his expression measured and under control.

"If you don't want to see me, then say so. But there's no need to ignore me and avoid my calls," Zach said, his eyes filling with fire.

"It isn't that I don't want to see you," Bull explained, his stomach tying itself in knots. "It's that I want you safe." He raked his gaze over Zach. "I need to know you're safe. If I could keep you with me all the time and watch over you day and night, I would." Bull shifted and tried to make it look like he was watching the crowded dance floor, but his attention was drawn to Zach. "They've approached me twice more, and each time they've become more and more insistent."

"Why you? Why can't they leave you alone and just find someone else?" Zach asked. "You have a life now and people who care about you." Zach stared at him, and Bull couldn't help smiling.

"These are people who care only for themselves and what they want. Others don't matter to them. Since they were born, everyone around them has given them everything they could possibly have asked for, so the concept of being told no only means they need to ask the question differently."

"So you've stayed away to protect me?" Zach asked. His grin was back. "You know, you could tell me when you decide things like that." Bull stared at him in complete surprise. "I'm not some weak little girl who needs protecting. I can take care of myself, and just so we're clear, I spent a good part of the time you were avoiding me wondering if you cared at all!" The music that had been pounding through the club suddenly stopped, and Zach's final words echoed through the space. The music started again, and Zach turned around and walked off, disappearing in the mass of people writhing and jumping on the dance floor.

"What the hell just happened?" Bull asked himself out loud.

"Maybe you need to talk to him instead of acting like a caveman." Bull looked down and saw Zach's friend Jeremy staring up at him. "He really cares about you." Jeremy took a step away, but then turned around. "If you care about someone, you don't make their decisions for them. You make the decisions together." Jeremy left, and Bull clenched his fists in frustration. He'd been trying to make sure nothing happened to Zach because the thought of him hurt scared Bull to death. Instead, it seemed Zach and his friends were angry at him for staying away.

Bull stayed where he was, though he wasn't really seeing what was happening around him. A fight broke out on the other side of the club, and it wasn't until the other bouncers broke it apart that he saw what was happening. Bull cursed under his breath and pushed all thought of Zach to the back of his mind. He had a job to do. That was what he was here for. Not to spend his time thinking of…. Bull's internal pep talk stopped like the needle on a record when he saw Zach dancing just a few feet away, moving and shaking his little behind. Zach didn't look at him, but Bull knew deep down this performance was for him.

The beat of the music slowed and so did Zach, gliding and weaving his body in erotic undulations that Bull could not look away from. His mouth went dry and he stared at Zach as he danced. The rest of the people in the club seemed to disappear, leaving only Zach moving his lithe body in flowing rhythms to the music. Bull stepped forward to where Zach danced and placed his hand on his shoulder. Zach stopped moving and turned toward him. "Was that little show for everyone, or just for me?"

Zach's gaze raked over him. "That dance was for the person who truly cares about me and my feelings. Is that you?" Zach challenged.

Bull reached down and cupped Zach's chin in his hand. "You know it is," Bull said.

"Then we do things together," Zach said. "I'm not asking to make your decisions for you, but I want you to talk to me before making decisions that affect us. And you staying away and keeping your distance definitely affects us."

"Okay," Bull agreed. "I'll try my best. But my judgment isn't as sound as it should be where you're concerned."

Zach moved closer, wrapped his arms around Bull's neck, and tugged him down. "If you don't think I would fight for you just as hard as you'd fight for me, you're full of shit."

Bull knew Zach thought he could fight for him, but these people would stomp Zach out if they thought it would get Bull to do what they wanted, and that thought alone was enough to make Bull's heart ache. However, it had been a very long time since anyone had said they'd fight for him. What mattered was the sentiment behind Zach's comment, rather than his actual ability to fight. "All right," Bull said, and Zach nodded, but didn't let go.

"I have one more question: Will you dance with me?" Zach asked.

"I'm supposed to be working," Bull said. "How about we dance together after I get home? You can put some music on and we'll dance privately." Bull leaned close. "When we're at home, I can actually strip you naked while we dance." Bull felt Zach shiver in his arms and he leaned in, kissing him hard before backing away. "I really need to try to concentrate on my work and I can't do that with you distracting me every few minutes."

"I know. I didn't intend to stay long. But I wanted you to know exactly what you'd been missing," Zach said with a mischievous smile.

"You're a minx, you know that?" Bull told him.

"And only you get to see it, just like I'm the only one who sees that you're one of the kindest men I've ever met," Zach whispered. "And don't worry, I have no intention of spreading that around or otherwise I'd have to fight the boys off you with a stick." Zach kissed him and then backed away. Bull watched him as he walked over to the table where his friends waited. Zach sat down, and they began talking. Bull turned away and was finally able to concentrate, at least for a few minutes.

Thankfully, Zach and his friends only stayed for another hour or so and then left. He made Zach promise not to be alone. He didn't tell him the exact reason, and thankfully Zach didn't ask.

"We're all going to Kevin's," Zach told him, "and then I'll come to your place and be waiting for you when you get done with work." Needless to say, the thought of Zach waiting for him at his place was enough to keep Bull on his toes the entire night and to rush the last people out of the club as soon as they closed. He helped Harry close up, trying to keep his impatience from showing.

As he left the club at the end of the night, Bull looked all around for any signs he might be watched. He didn't feel like he was, but that might only mean he hadn't picked up on it.

"Are you going to be okay?" Harry asked as Bull checked over his car before unlocking it and getting inside. "I can follow you home if you need me to."

"No, I'm just being paranoid." Granted, that paranoia had helped keep him alive in the past. "I'll see you before opening." Bull drove directly home. The streets were largely deserted at this hour. He'd be able to spot anyone following him a mile away, and if someone had been watching him, they'd know where he was going at this hour. He turned the radio on low and drove.

Bull finally pulled into his driveway and turned off the engine. All night, whenever his mind was idle, which was more often than usual, he'd thought about Zach waiting for him when he got home. Low lights burned in the kitchen and living room. He wasn't sure if he'd find Zach waiting for him in bed or asleep on the sofa, but he smiled as he got out of the car and unlocked the back door. His mother had been gone a week, and to his surprise he missed her a little. Things had changed. He wasn't sure if it was permanent, but it was definitely a start, and largely thanks to Zach.

The scent of strong coffee reached his nose as soon as he opened the door. He stepped inside, closed the door, and walked into the kitchen. "Zach, you didn't...." Bull stopped midsentence when he saw Junior's father, Sheik Rashad, sitting at his table with a coffee cup in front of him. "Where's Zach?" Bull asked without any sort of preamble.

"Your little friend is fine," Rashad said, but his eyes spelled out the unsaid "for now." He sipped from the cup and then set it back down with the slightest ting. "Would you like some? I brought it from home. I thought it might help bring back memories for you."

"No," Bull said, watching Rashad as he pulled out his chair. "Why are you here?"

"Because you have repeatedly turned down my generous offers of employment," he said matter-of-factly.

Bull glanced around the kitchen and then out into the living room. Lights flickered in the other room. The television had been left on, but with the sound muted. He could see the sofa, but it was empty. "Where is Zach?" he asked slowly.

"He has not been harmed, I assure you," Rashad told him. "We have more important things to talk about than your... little dalliance." He lifted the cup one more time. "I came here to speak with you man to man, with no intermediaries to get in the way." He sipped and set down the cup. When he turned back toward him, Bull saw something he'd never seen in the always confident and assured sheik before: fear. Bone-deep, panic-inducing fear. He hid it well, but he couldn't hide it from Bull.

"It's a long way to travel to offer someone a job," Bull said. "Why is this so important that you'd send multiple messages and have people watching me? I'm not in the business any longer. I haven't done any jobs since the one that resulted in Junior's death." He kept his voice level and as cool as he could. "And I don't intend to do any more. I have a life here now, and there are many other people who can do the job you need."

"That's where you are wrong," Rashad said, his accent becoming thicker, the only indication of his frustration. "I owe you a great debt for saving the life of me and my son. Junior threw away that gift through his stubbornness. But I have not, and I need the services of the man who saved my life once." He paused and swallowed. "I need that man to protect the life he saved."

Bull paused to clear his head. He was exhausted, but he needed to keep his mind sharp. "Why do you need protecting? You have a team of bodyguards and an around-the-clock security detail. What difference could I make?"

"My security detail has been infiltrated. The traitor has been rooted out and taken care of," Rashad said. "However, the group that killed my son has grown and shifted into a terrorist group that is now forging links with others. They must be eliminated before they can pose a threat to my country and my entire family."

Bull stared at the sheik, his mind divided between what he was being told and his concern over Zach. Was he still in the house, or had Rashad taken him somewhere to be used as leverage? He did believe Rashad was telling him the truth and that Zach was unharmed. Rashad's pride would not allow him to lie so baldly. He might prevaricate, though. "Is this threat because of the raid that killed your son?"

Rashad didn't nod or answer at first. "That unfortunate incident might have been the catalyst for a number of the issues facing my country. You understand my country and my family." The sheik's gaze faltered. "You were part of my family once." Bull nodded. That had ended with the initial discovery of his relationship with Junior. "And once you are family, you are always family, even when the head of that family acts rashly out of pain and pride."

Bull nodded his understanding of the implications Rashad was suggesting. "I am still the same person I was then, and the man you found here in my house means as much to me as your son did." Rashad's expression shifted, as if the coffee had just turned bitter. "I know you don't understand, either by will or inability, but things between your son and me were not how you think they were. It was deeper than merely physical."

Rashad sighed, some of the fire leaving his eyes, but he retained his rigid posture. "That is not possible."

"You might not think so, but nonetheless they were. I deeply cared for Junior, and he hurt me when he left."

"He returned to his family and his obligations," Rashad said, his words measured.

Bull knew there was little hope of ever getting the conservative sheik to understand, but he had to try one last time. "I know that you loved Junior's mother very deeply. According to what Junior told me, the two of you were a love match. He told me his mother lit up whenever the two of you were in the same room." Bull watched Rashad's expression. "I can see that it's true."

"Yes, it was. I still mourn her passing."

Bull nodded very slowly. He was treading on quicksand. "What would your life have been like if she had not been part of it? Would you have been as happy and contented for the time you had her? Would your heart have rejoiced every day if she had not held part of it?"

"No," Rashad admitted.

"Then why is it so hard for you to accept that Junior might have felt the same way for me, and I for him? I know this is very foreign to your way of thinking, but what if it's true anyway?" Bull decided to press on. "I know you are a wise and thoughtful man. So I'm asking you to try to understand that I cannot work for you any longer. I watched a person I cared for die in front of me. I did not

135

mourn him openly out of respect for his memory and your family. I did my mourning out of sight. But returning to your country, fighting the same battle that killed Junior over again, is not something I'm willing or able to do." Bull sighed. "What we started all those years ago was a mistake. You and your people are still paying for that mistake in deaths and lost sons."

Rashad slowly rose to his feet, and Bull stood as well. "There is nothing I can do to convince you?"

"Short of taking an action that would make you my enemy, no," Bull said. He extended his hand, and Rashad hesitated before taking it. "I will share what I've learned: the best form of security is peace."

"I wonder if that is possible," Rashad said.

"I don't know either, but if it is possible, then you're the one person who can show the way," Bull told him. "You care for your people and have their respect. You lost your son to this conflict, so maybe if you're willing to forgive, then others will be as well." Bull's heart pounded.

"You should have been a diplomat rather than a soldier," Rashad said.

Bull shook his head. "Thank you," he said calmly. Rashad pulled out his phone and made a quick call, speaking in Arabic. Then he hung up, and Bull walked him to the door. A limousine pulled into the drive. It stopped, and a man held the door for Rashad. Bull saw him pause for a second, their gazes meeting.

"Your small friend is inside and unharmed." Rashad nodded and then ducked into the car, followed by his security man. The car then backed out of the drive and sped away.

As soon as they were gone, Bull raced back inside and through the house. He found Zach asleep on top of his bed with the spread curled around him. "Sweetheart," Bull said, sitting on the edge of the bed. He lightly kissed Zach's forehead and Zach blinked. "Are you okay?" Bull pulled him into a hug. "I thought you might have been hurt." The things that had gone through his mind at first had scared him to death.

"Why? What happened?" Zach asked, and Bull inhaled deeply and sighed. Zach had no idea anyone had been in the house.

"Nothing," Bull said. "I'll tell you all about it later." He covered Zach's mouth with his, kissing him hard, listening as Zach's moans became louder and more insistent by the second. Zach panted when they broke the kiss. "Let me lock up the house and I'll be right back." Bull checked all the doors before returning to the bedroom. Zach had rolled over, and his butt stuck out from under the bedspread. Bull smiled and stripped off his clothes before straightening the bedding and helping Zach get under the covers. Then he did the same. Zach inched back until they pressed together. He mumbled something Bull couldn't understand and then went quiet, almost instantly falling back to sleep. Bull closed his eyes and followed right behind him.

"BULL'S RESIDENCE." Bull woke to Zach talking.

"This is Zach," he heard him say. Bull opened his eyes and saw Zach sitting up in bed, talking on the phone. He hadn't even heard it ring. "I'll get him for you." A pause. "Oh, okay," Zach said, sounding wary. Bull groaned as he sat up and watched as Zach listened to whoever was on the phone. "That's very nice. I'd like that." Zach smiled. "Yes, he's right here. I think he just woke up." Zach covered the mouthpiece with his hand. "I grabbed for the phone to let you sleep. I hope it's okay."

"Of course," Bull said, blinking.

Zach passed him the phone. "It's your mother."

Bull stifled a groan before knitting his brows together, wondering why Zach was so happy. "Hello," he said groggily.

"You never call," his mother said, happily. She sounded *happy*.

"Sorry. I've been busy for the past week." Boy, had he ever. "What's up?"

"Your stepfather and I have decided to try to patch things up," his mother said. "We've both done and said things we wished we hadn't. So we've decided to reconcile, date, and see what happens."

"I'm glad you're happy," Bull said.

"It sounds like someone else is happy too," she said and then giggled. His mother never giggled. Bull checked the caller ID just to make sure. "That's a very good thing."

"Okay, who are you and what have you done with my mother?" Bull asked. "I take it things have changed for you?" Bull lay back and let his eyes drift closed as he listened.

"Yes. You were right, damn it," she said. "I asked some of my friends here, and they said the same thing you did." She didn't sound very pleased.

"Mom, it's good. You can fix it," Bull said. "And you'll be happier because of it." The covers that had pooled around his waist slipped away and Zach stretched across his lap. Bull shivered when he felt Zach's lips slide along his cock, which perked up instantly. "I'm on the phone to my mother," Bull whispered, covering the mouthpiece.

"Mr. Happy doesn't seem to care," Zach said and then sucked the head between his lips. Bull stifled a groan, rolled his eyes, and tried to listen to what his mother had to say.

"I really think that I will be," she said.

"That's great," Bull said, gritting his teeth to keep from moaning loudly into his mother's ear. "I think in a few months, once it gets colder here, Zach and I will plan a trip to come see you." Zach sucked him hard, and Bull inhaled deeply, releasing his breath slowly so his mother wouldn't know he was getting the blowjob of his life. "Mom, I have to go. I need to sleep a while longer and then get a few things done before work. I'll call you in a few hours." He was trying desperately to keep from screaming his lungs out.

"Okay, we'll talk soon," she said and disconnected the call.

Bull tossed the phone onto the bed. "You're in such trouble," he said, threading his fingers through Zach's soft hair.

"Do you want me to stop?" Zach asked. He then sucked him deep and hard, driving any remark Bull might have been able to make from his mind, not that Bull minded in the least.

"Jesus, what you do to me," Bull groaned. Zach didn't answer, at least not in words, as he bobbed his pretty head on Bull's cock.

Bull slowly slid down the mattress, and Zach went right along with him. Once he was lying flat, Bull nudged Zach around until he straddled his head. Then he guided Zach lower and returned the favor. Zach stilled and hummed throatily as Bull sucked him.

"Bull," Zach said quietly. "It's too much."

Bull patted Zach's butt, and he shifted to the side. Bull sat up and kissed Zach hard, then positioned him on the bed. Then he ran his hand down his back and over his butt. "Spread your legs farther apart."

"Bull," Zach said self-consciously. Bull kissed Zach's cheek and stroked down his spread crack, teasing the flesh of his opening. Zach hissed softly and moaned. Bull licked his cheek and moved closer. "What are you doing? Oh my God!" Zach cried.

Bull licked him, then sucked his tender flesh, Zach's intense musk bursting on his tongue. "Like that?" he asked.

"You bet your ass," Zach told him, and Bull tried to keep from laughing. Zach never swore, at least not like that. Bull returned to licking and tasting, listening as Zach slowly went to pieces. He shook, vibrated, and made whimpery sounds, clutching the bedding so tightly a few times Bull swore it was going to tear. "Please, Bull, don't make me wait anymore."

Bull straightened up and reached over to the bedside table for a condom and some lube. After thorough preparation that elicited more moans that drove Bull halfway to heaven, he slowly pressed into Zach's body.

He'd fucked many men in his life, most of them nameless and faceless, but he'd know Zach's body anywhere. Bull stroked Zach's smooth butt as he soothed him, waiting for the telltale high-pitched moan that told him Zach was ready. Then he began to move as slowly as his passion-fevered mind would allow. After a few minutes, he pulled out and helped Zach roll over. He'd never really cared if he could see the people he was having sex with, but while making love to Zach, he felt a need. He had to see into his eyes, watch as they widened or glazed over with passion, or see his mouth hang open as he came.

They moved together with what was becoming practiced ease. "I could love on you forever," Bull said. Zach gasped and stilled completely. Bull wondered if something was wrong and stopped as well. "Did I hurt you?"

"No," Zach said. "You said love for the first time."

"Oh," Bull said as fear ran up his spine. "Is that bad?"

"No." Zach grinned. "It's good. Really good." Zach reached forward and tugged him down, holding Bull around the neck while he kissed him. "Because I love you too."

Now it was Bull's turn to still. "You do?" He stroked Zach's cheek.

"Of course I do. If I didn't, I wouldn't have been mad at you for not calling me." Zach rolled his eyes and then grinned. "Sometimes you're a bit of a yutz." Bull slowly withdrew and pushed back into Zach. That smile faded, and the impending giggle morphed into a long, deep moan.

"Now who's a yutz?" Bull countered, changing the angle so there was no way Zach could answer. Talk was overrated and Bull decided it was time to let his body do the talking. He thrust faster, making Zach moan and whimper. All attempts at conversation ended as they moved together. The bed shook and might have banged the wall a few times. Zach's moans changed into deep groans and then yells of passion that echoed off the walls. The moans turned to pleading for release. As Bull felt his own climax nearing, he stroked Zach hard and fast. Zach rolled his head back and forth on the pillow, mumbling something completely incoherent, until his entire body tensed. Bull stroked faster, plunging harder into Zach's body until he felt him start to come. Bull followed right behind, and the entire world held still.

Bull opened his eyes, and Zach stared back at him. It could only have been a few seconds, but it seemed wonderfully longer. Zach had told him he loved him. Only one other person had done so in recent memory. "What is it?" Zach asked. "You look pale."

"I'm fine," Bull whispered.

"No, you're not," Zach countered and stared at him. "How long has it been since someone told you they loved you?" Bull didn't answer. "It was Junior, wasn't it?"

Bull nodded. "Before that it was my dad."

"Having someone tell you they love you doesn't mean they're going to die," Zach said. Bull knew it had to be a guess on Zach's part, but he'd hit the nail on the head. "I love you," Zach repeated.

Bull swallowed and hoped to God Zach was right.

CHAPTER EIGHT

BULL HAD fallen back to sleep, and Zach watched him for a while before getting out of bed and leaving the room. Bull needed his rest, and Zach didn't want to keep him up. Thankfully, he didn't have to go to work. He had no plans for the day and he hoped Bull didn't either. Zach located the small bag he'd brought with him and pulled on a pair of sweatpants and a T-shirt.

He went to the living room and turned on Bull's television, keeping the volume low. He got comfortable and let himself become engrossed in *Hot in Cleveland*.

"What's so funny?" Bull asked, rubbing his eyes as he wandered into the room naked.

"I'm glad the curtains are closed; otherwise we'd have a stampede," Zach said as he stood up. "They'd want you for themselves, but I don't share."

Bull wrapped his arms around him, and Zach hummed contentedly. "I don't share either," Bull growled deep and long. Zach shivered as Bull slid his warm hands down his back, then pushed his sweats down his hips until they pooled on the floor. Zach stepped out of them, and Bull placed his hands under Zach's butt and hoisted him upward. Zach wrapped his legs around Bull's waist. Bull kissed him hard, turned around, and carried him back to the bedroom. Bull laid him on the bed and stilled. Zach wondered if something was wrong.

"I've been to war, looked the enemy in the eyes. I've seen things that would make most men gouge their eyes out," Bull said. "I'm afraid of very little, but the thought of being without you scares me to death. I can yell, scream, use my voice to stop a tank, but telling you how I feel seems impossible."

"You don't have to say anything you aren't ready for," Zach said, stroking Bull's cheek. "I know how you feel about me."

"But you deserve to hear me say it. I'm not going to be one of those guys who gets mushy all the time. I don't wear my heart on my sleeve, but you deserve to hear me say how I feel." Bull stroked his cheek, and Zach locked his gaze onto Bull's. His heart pounded as he waited for what Bull had to say. "I love you, Zach."

"I love you too," Zach said. Closing his eyes, he tugged Bull down to him. They kissed, and this time Zach took charge. Bull's lips parted, and Zach surged his tongue forward, taking possession of Bull's mouth, letting him know just how special he felt. When Bull moaned softly, Zach smiled against his lips.

"What?" Bull asked, pulling away slightly.

"I like that I can make you sound like that," Zach said, pulling him back into a kiss.

They made love quietly and deeply. Zach loved when Bull got energetic, but he also loved slow, intimate movements. The headboard didn't bang, the bed only swayed a little, but Zach's body tingled with desire and his cock throbbed and jumped, bouncing against his stomach as he held on as long as he possibly could. Bull held him tight as Zach plunged over the edge, and this time he felt Bull throb deep inside him.

Zach sighed and closed his eyes, holding Bull tight as afterglow flowed over him. He didn't want to move. Everything was perfect right now, and he wanted it to last. Zach shivered slightly when their bodies separated, but he didn't move until Bull got out of bed and gently helped him into the bathroom. He turned on the water, and they stepped into the shower. Bull took up most of the space, which meant Zach had to stay close. That was fine with him. Bull faced the shower, and Zach held him around the waist, resting

143

against him. The proximity to Bull's skin was already having an effect.

"You are a minx," Bull said as he slowly turned around.

Zach looked down at his dick, already pointing toward Bull, and then raised his gaze and smiled. "Do you think that someday I might get to...." He swallowed, wondering how Bull would react. "... do you?"

Bull pulled him close. "It isn't something I really enjoy, or haven't in the past, but yes, I'd like you to make love to me." Bull kissed him, and Zach moaned, the water cascading over them.

ZACH HAD intended to make breakfast after their shower, but that got delayed a number of times. By the time they left the bedroom, they were both starving. Bull took him out to lunch, which was interrupted by a phone call, and then dropped him at his apartment in the afternoon. Bull had said he had some errands to run, but he followed Zach inside.

"I thought you had things to do?" Zach asked.

"I do, but...." Bull sat down and Zach's old sofa creaked slightly. "I have a confession to make, and I hope you aren't going to be angry with me."

Zach lowered himself in a chair, wondering what was wrong.

"A few weeks ago, after I met your uncle, I called a few people from my unit who are now in law enforcement."

"Bull," Zach said, his stomach roiling. "What did you do?"

"I didn't do anything other than ask them to take a look into your uncle's behavior. He isn't normal. That call I got at lunch, when I stepped away from the table, was from one of my contacts. I didn't tell you then because I thought it better that you hear this in private." Bull paused, and Zach leaned forward, wishing he'd just tell him. "They've built a case, and your uncle is going to be arrested."

"Oh," Zach said. "I guess I wasn't the only person he beat when they displeased him."

Bull leaned forward and reached out to touch Zach's leg. "Your uncle is being arrested primarily for arson and murder."

"I don't...." Zach gasped. "Are you saying...?" Zach stilled as his heart beat in his ears. "Is this because of my parents?"

"Yes. The story you told me about the way your parents died rubbed me the wrong way. It was too simplistic and convenient. So I passed your story on to some friends with keen investigative skills. It seems your uncle had a lot of ways to keep people from leaving his sphere of influence. He coerced people, beat them like he did you, and God knows what else. But none of those things were working on your parents. It's all coming out now, but it seems your parents were getting ready to leave, and your uncle couldn't have that. If his relatives left, then others would as well."

"So he burned down their house with them in it?" Zach could barely speak as the grief he'd carried for so long welled back to the surface.

"It appears so. I don't have any details because it's an open case, and some of what I just told you I shouldn't even know. But this is too important for me to keep quiet about." Bull knelt next to Zach's chair, and Zach reached out, throwing himself at him.

"What am I going to do?"

"Answer the agents' questions and testify at your uncle's trial regarding how you were treated. I know this is hard, but at least you know now. There had to be some suspicion in the back of your mind just from the way you told me the story. Now you know the truth."

Zach blinked. "The bastard," he swore. "He took everything away from me, even them!" He clenched his fists tightly.

"I'm sorry I didn't tell you earlier, but I didn't know that anything would come of it." Bull held him tightly. "I do love you."

"I know," Zach whispered.

"I hope it helps," Bull said.

145

Zach held him tighter. "It helps a lot," he croaked and then buried his head against Bull's shoulder and cried. How long he stayed that way, he wasn't sure. The tears eventually dried, but he held Bull anyway, needing to be close to him. "It seems stupid to be grieving over all this again. They've been gone for a while, and I've moved on."

"No, it's not—thinking your folks died in an accident is very different from knowing they were deliberately hurt," Bull told him. "I've seen a lot of people die in my life. I've killed people. It was war, and that was my job. Sometimes I can see the people I've killed in my sleep. But I've never hurt anyone who wasn't out to hurt me first. I know it might not be much of a distinction, but…."

"It is. It means you're the man I fell in love with," Zach said, closing his eyes and hugging Bull tighter. After a while he straightened up, wiping his eyes with the heel of his hand. "I'm sorry. You had things you needed to do."

"I can do them later," Bull said.

"No, it's okay. I need some time alone to think. Go run your errands—just come back when you're done." Zach swallowed and Bull stood up. "I'll be fine."

"You're sure? I can always get Harry to do them for me," Bull said.

Zach shook his head. "Go on. I'll be fine."

Bull gave him a gentle kiss and slowly went to the door, looking back to him one last time before he left the apartment. Zach smiled and made "scoot" motions with his hands. Bull closed the door, and Zach sat alone, staring at the blank television screen.

His mind raced. Bull was right: he'd had suspicions about his uncle, but he hadn't wanted to believe or even contemplate them. Who wanted to think a relative, someone he'd known all his life, was a murderer? Zach curled up on the sofa, resting his head on the arm. He'd told his uncle he was free and he'd meant it. But his freedom had come at a high cost. His family, friends, and now his parents' deaths—all of it was linked to his quest to get away and live his own life. "I'm sorry," Zach said quietly into the empty room. He

146

wasn't expecting a response and didn't get one. Thank goodness, or otherwise he'd be nuts.

Zach sat unmoving on the sofa and eventually closed his eyes. Being alone like this probably wasn't a good idea. Yeah, it gave him time to think, but what ran though his mind were things it was probably best he didn't think about all at once. But everything—guilt, second-guessed decisions, insisting his parents simply come with him—all of it rolled over in his mind again and again. He wondered what Bull would tell him, what sort of advice the former soldier and mercenary would give him to deal with the guilt.

He reached over to the coffee table, grabbed the remote, and turned on the television for some company. He watched some sitcom reruns and soon his attention wavered. He closed his eyes and willed everything to go away. Not that it worked, but he eventually relaxed enough to doze off.

He woke to heavy footsteps outside his door. Zach shifted and waited for Bull to come in. The door opened, and Zach looked up before jumping to his feet. "What are you doing here?" Zach asked his uncle, taking a step back. He should have locked the door.

"I knew you were behind all this," his uncle spat as he pushed the apartment door closed. "I knew you were the one who spread all those lies about me setting that fire."

"What fire?" Zach asked, having the presence of mind to play dumb.

"Don't take me for a fool," his uncle said, stepping closer. "I have friends. I know what's going on. I know that... that... abomination you fornicate with called in some favors and had me investigated. Me!" he yelled. "People like you are the ones who should be investigated and locked away forever."

"That's enough," Zach said forcefully. "I'm not some child, and I won't take your crap. Leave." Zach pointed toward the door. He wondered if his uncle was carrying a gun. His eyes were wide and crazed. "You have no place here. We're no longer family—isn't that what you told me? Well, I agree. You aren't my family," Zach said slowly and firmly. "I disown you! You're nothing at all to me, and I don't care what happens to you."

His uncle stilled. Zach took another step back to put a little more distance between them. "They've all left me. I was the leader, their moral compass, and they threw me out, cast me aside."

Zach shrugged. It was impossible for him to feel sorry for the man who'd murdered his parents. But he needed to keep his uncle calm. His uncle looked crazy, and Zach had no idea what he'd do. "I'm sorry they left you," he lied through his teeth. "No one should be left all alone in the world."

"No. Well, no upstanding person should be alone," his uncle said, clearly taking a swipe at Zach.

"So why did you come here? What do you want from me? I have no idea what's going on or why everyone seems to have left you."

"Don't lie to me," his uncle hissed and moved closer once again. "I know you know everything. Like I said, I have friends, and you, boy, put your boyfriend up to having me investigated."

"When have I ever lied to you?" Zach countered. "In all the years you've known me, since I was five years old, have I ever lied to you?" Zach stared at him, and his uncle paused. "I told you the truth always, even when I knew I was going to get a beating for it. Hell, you whipped me for telling you the truth, so don't you call me a liar. You're the liar!" Rage welled inside Zach, cascading through him. He clenched his fists and moved closer to his uncle, drawing himself up as tall as he could. "You were my family and you turned on me because I was gay. That's not family, that's sick."

"Don't talk to me about sick, boy," his uncle sneered.

"I'll talk to you about anything I want. This is my apartment." Zach reached into his pocket for his phone, but it wasn't there. He glanced around and saw it on the edge of the coffee table. "Like I said, it's best if you leave right now."

"I'm not going anywhere. You turned everyone against me and you're going to pay." His uncle reached for his belt, unhooked it, and pulled it off.

"What, you think you're going to whip me like you did when I was a kid?" Zach asked, standing his ground.

"You're still a boy, and I know I can beat the Lord back into you," his uncle said, spittle flying everywhere. Zach wouldn't have been surprised to see him start foaming at the mouth.

"I told you before. You will not touch me," Zach told him. His uncle doubled the belt and reached for Zach's wrist. "Stop it. Now!" Zach called, but his uncle kept coming.

Out of the corner of his eye, Zach saw the apartment door open and Bull step inside. His uncle reached for him, trying to grab his wrist. Zach screamed and kicked, sweeping his uncle's feet out from under him. "You stupid ass," Zach cried as he kicked his uncle in the side. "I took self-defense classes because of you." Zach kicked him again. "I learned how to fight because of your sorry ass." Zach aimed for his uncle's head, but Bull grabbed him from behind and held him tight. "And no one is going to hurt me again!" He struggled to get away.

"It's okay," Bull whispered in his ear. "He's down and he's not going to hurt you again." Zach stopped struggling and stared at his uncle, who lay curled up on the floor, moaning like a two-dollar whore. Bull released him, and Zach stepped away, reached over to the coffee table, and scooped up his phone. He pressed 911.

"I want to report an assault," Zach said when someone answered. The operator asked for his name and address and what happened. "My uncle broke into my apartment and tried to assault me, so I kicked his ass into next week. You should send someone now, because if he gets up, I'll kick his sorry ass again. Oh, and the uncle in question is wanted for murder." Zach stared at his uncle as he hung up the phone. "Yeah, I know everything." He looked at Bull before standing as close to his uncle as he dared. The urge to kick his face in would be too strong to resist if he got too close. "I know what you did, and so does everyone at home. You're going away for a long time, and I intend to testify against you the first chance I get."

"It's okay," Bull told him again. "Everything's going to be fine. He's not going anywhere, and no one is going to hurt you when I'm around." Bull tightened his embrace.

"Okay. But if he gets up, I get to beat the shit out of him," Zach said.

"That's a deal. If there's any beating to be done, you get to do it."

"You're humoring me," Zach asked.

"Are you kidding? I saw what you did to him. I'm staying out of it." Bull chuckled, and Zach sighed and settled in his embrace. The sirens got louder, and Zach waited for the police to enter.

As soon as they did, the apartment became a hive of activity, questions, and more questions. They took statements from him, Bull, and his uncle before cuffing the older man and hauling him away. It seemed he'd gotten out of Lancaster just ahead of the police, and they were more than happy to have him in custody.

"He says he wants to press charges," an officer told Zach.

"Let him." Zach turned around and lifted his shirt. "He did this to me, and he killed my parents. I think he deserved whatever I did to him."

"He had a gun in his car. We don't know if he planned to use it, but it was loaded and hidden beneath the seat," the officer explained. "He doesn't seem particularly stable at the moment, so who knows what's going through his head."

"I understand, but don't let him off because of it," Zach said firmly.

"Unfortunately, that sort of thing is for the lawyers and courts," the officer said with resignation, and Zach nodded. He knew that, but he had to say it. His uncle was off his nut, but Zach was convinced he knew what he was doing and vowed to testify as many times as he needed to make a jury believe it.

"Here's my card. I'll be in touch if anything happens, but based upon your statements, I doubt he can make any charges stick," the officer said.

Zach took the card and clutched it between his fingers. "Please call if there's anything I can do."

The officer promised that he would and left the apartment. Zach closed the door and made it to the sofa before his legs buckled underneath him.

"Zach," Bull said as he rushed toward him.

"I'm okay. I just can't believe I actually attacked my uncle." Zach held his head in his hands.

"You didn't. He attacked you, and you defended yourself," Bull told him. "There's nothing wrong with that at all. When I came in and saw him coming at you, I was prepared to take him out, but I didn't have to. You defended yourself." Bull wrapped him in his arms, and Zach closed his eyes, still shuddering. "Where did you learn to fight like that?"

"After I left home, I was pretty messed up. I'd lost my family, though I know now that I was a victim. I didn't then." Zach looked up into Bull's eyes. "On one of the bulletin boards at school, I saw a class being offered in self-defense for women. I went, and while initially they wouldn't let me into the class, I explained to the instructor what had happened to me." Zach swallowed. "Believe it or not, she polled the class, and they voted me in." Zach blinked. "Most of them had experienced something similar to what I'd gone through." Zach sighed and swallowed hard as he remembered how much in common he'd had with all those women. "It was a basic class, but it gave me confidence so I could stop feeling like a victim. I wish I could find the instructor now and tell her that she truly helped me."

"I bet she already knows," Bull said. "I helped teach a class like that a few years ago, and you can see the change in people when they no longer feel helpless. That's the real accomplishment, because you won't use what you learned if you don't feel confidence in yourself. And you learned that lesson well."

Zach felt Bull shake slightly and he pulled back so he could look at him. "What's wrong?"

"I almost lost you again," Bull whispered.

"What do you mean by 'again'?" Zach asked.

"Last night I thought something had happened to you when I came home and Rashad was in the house. Now I walk in here and

151

your uncle is attacking you," Bull said. "I'm starting to wonder if you aren't the superhero."

Zach scoffed lightly and swatted Bull's chest. "I can't be a superhero. I don't look like one. You're the superhero." He rested his head on Bull's shoulder. "I know you don't like to see yourself as comforting, but you are to me."

"I want to be comforting for you." Bull slowly rubbed his back, and the tension began to drain from Zach's muscles. "And you are the superhero. Never doubt that." Zach lifted his head to make sure Bull wasn't kidding. "Look what you've done. I was the biggest hardass on earth, and you got me to open my heart to you. You stood up to the man who abused you and"—Bull paused—"killed your parents. You even stood up to my mother, and I'd like to think that's part of the reason she's trying to change. You bring out the good in people."

"I didn't in my uncle," Zach countered.

"Your uncle is nuts; he doesn't count," Bull retorted, and Zach chuckled softly. "You make people want to be happy. After all you've been through, you're still able to smile." Bull hugged him close. "That makes you a superhero to me."

"I can live with that," Zach said, closing his eyes as he enjoyed the warmth of Bull's embrace. "When do you need to go to work? I know you can't stay home tonight. It's busy and not fair to Harry."

"I need to leave in a few hours, but I don't want to leave you alone." Zach opened his mouth to protest, but Bull silenced him with a finger. "I'll spend the entire night worrying about you."

"I could call the guys and see if they want to go to the club?" Zach asked and then yawned. "Maybe that isn't such a good idea." He hadn't slept well, and he needed to get up for work in the morning.

"Call your friends and see if some of them can come over. I know you should be fine, but sometimes people beat the system, and if your uncle is released on bail, I want you safe."

"Okay. I'll call them," Zach said. He sighed and reached for his phone to make the calls. The guys were excited to get together. Jeremy invited everyone over to his place at seven, so Zach had a few hours with Bull before he needed to get ready to leave and Bull had to go to work.

Bull sat on the sofa, and once Zach was done with his calls, he straddled Bull's legs and sat on his lap. Bull tugged Zach's shirt out of his pants and pulled it up and over his head. "I need to see you're okay."

Zach shivered as Bull checked him over using his lips and tongue. "You taste the same," Bull mumbled against his belly. Zach giggled slightly, but that soon morphed into a soft groan. "You really are okay," Bull said.

"Yes, and feeling better all the time." Zach groaned as Bull sucked a nipple. He leaned back, feeling safe cradled in Bull's hands.

"I think we should take this... examination... into the other room," Bull suggested. Zach climbed off his lap, and Bull took his hand and led him to his bedroom. Bull stepped inside, took one look at his small bed, and turned back to him. "I'm afraid we'll break it. Either that or we'll end up on the floor." Bull led him back to the living room. He pulled the curtains and then pressed Zach back onto the cushions.

He proceeded to strip Zach naked, then tasted and sucked him until Zach could barely see or think. By the time they were done, Zach lay on top of Bull's sprawled body. The coffee table had been pushed to the other side of the room, the old rug on the floor was askew, the entire room smelled of sex, and there were pillows and cushions strewn everywhere. Zach was sore in the best way possible. He groaned softly, shifting on his warm cushion.

"As much as I want to stay here with you forever, I need to get to the club," Bull whispered.

"And I need to get to Jeremy's or they'll rib me all night." Zach shifted to the floor and slowly got to his feet. "Not that they won't already. It seems my sex life has become quite the topic of conversation." Bull huffed softly. "Yeah, well, they keep wondering if Bull is a nickname or a description." Zach giggled. "I haven't had the heart to tell them it's both. Besides, they'd be jealous and try to steal you away." He chuckled again. "Not that they aren't already

153

jealous." He began picking up his clothes. "Would you care to tell me how my pants made it onto the curtain rod?"

"I got a little energetic," Bull quipped and then smiled. "So sue me."

Zach jumped to grab the leg of his pants. He managed to hook them and pull them down. "Next time, get energetic with your own pants." Zach hurried back to the bathroom and cleaned up quickly. Then he got dressed and joined Bull in the living room.

"I'll stop at home and clean up before I go to work." Bull sniffed slightly. "I smell like you, and while that's a nice thing, I don't need to spend the night at work smelling like sex."

"There are worse things," Zach said as he grabbed his wallet and keys. He followed Bull out and locked the door before happily descending the stairs, watching Bull's butt in his jeans. He didn't hide his smile when Bull looked over his shoulder, and he didn't shift his gaze from Bull's meaty posterior. "You watch mine all the time," Zach said before pushing through the door.

Before separating to go to their cars, Bull kissed him lightly and extracted a promise that he'd call when he got to Jeremy's *and* he'd call when he got home. Zach rolled his eyes, but promised anyway before getting in his car and heading right over to Jeremy's.

"SO WHY is there a bruise on your wrist?" Tristan said as they sat around the living room of the apartment Jeremy and Tristan shared. "Did Bull do that?"

Zach checked both wrists, shocked to see that one was indeed turning purple. It hurt, too, but he hadn't noticed it. "No. My uncle showed up."

"Are you okay?" Kevin asked, shoving away the bowl of Cheetos.

"Yeah," Zach said and gave them the condensed version of what happened. "He grabbed my wrist, and I laid him out." Zach smiled. "Then I kicked his ass."

"Yeah, right," Tristan said.

154

"I did. He came at me, and I went postal. I beat the crap out of him. Bull held me to calm me down. It was awesome." He truly felt free. The ghost of his uncle was gone, put to rest forever. He didn't tell his friends about his parents. He wasn't ready to talk about that yet, but he'd tell them eventually. "So let's celebrate.

"What, you kicking an old guy's ass?" Kevin joked as he reached for his beer.

"No. The fact that the old guy who beat me and lorded over my family and the rest of the people I knew growing up is finally getting his." Zach raised his soda can. He'd already had a beer and he was going to have to drive later. They clinked their cans and beer bottles before drinking.

With that out of the way, the conversation descended to their usual topics: comics, television, and, of course, guys. They talked of going to the club so Bull could let them in, but they all had to work the next day. They ended up watching television and gabbing until it was time to leave. He drove home and walked through his empty apartment. Zach called Bull and left a message when the call went to voice mail. He ended up packing a bag and leaving again, this time driving over to Bull's. He smiled as he used the key Bull had given him and let himself in. He set his bag in the bedroom, then went back to the living room and turned on the television. The club closed early on Sunday nights, and he figured he'd wait up for Bull, but ended up falling asleep.

He started awake when Bull kissed him.

"I wasn't expecting you to be here," Bull whispered.

"I missed you," Zach explained, barely opening his eyes. Bull gathered him into his arms, lifted Zach off the sofa, and carried him through the house and into the bedroom, where he placed him on the bed. Zach pulled off his shirt and scrambled under the covers. He felt Bull remove his shoes and pants. Bull joined him a few minutes later, and Zach snuggled up to him, falling back to sleep almost instantly.

CHAPTER NINE

BULL WOKE. The room was still dark, and he glanced at the clock beside the bed. Something was wrong. Instantly he knew someone else was in the house. Bull got up and pulled on jeans, then grabbed his gun from his dresser drawer and tucked it in the back of his jeans. He took a quick look at Zach and quietly left the bedroom. He walked silently through the house, avoiding every place on the floor that made a creak.

"What the hell is it with you coming in my house?" Bull asked when he got to the kitchen, staring at Spook, who was sitting at his table. He relaxed slightly.

"We have a little unfinished business," Spook said, standing up and pointing a gun at him. Bull groaned at his mistake, set his gun on the floor, and slowly moved to the center of the room. Bull shook his head and glared at the smaller man. "This was supposed to be an easy job. I get you to do the work for my client, and I get paid. It's that simple. Only you're too stubborn to take what was offered. I don't get paid, so I figure you need to pay me."

"Bullshit. I'm not giving you anything," Bull said. "Now get out of my house and don't come back. I've had it with everyone deciding what I'm going to do, and if you were dumb enough to take a job without getting paid up front, then you're the one who's stupid, not me."

"The deal was too good to pass up, and now I get nothing," Spook said, coming closer. "So just make it easy on both of us and pay up."

"No. Go back to Rashad and get the money from him. He has piles of it." Out of the corner of his eye, Bull saw movement down the hall. Shit, Zach was awake. Bull slowly worked his way toward the other side of the room, trying to get Spook's back to Zach. "I'm not going to give you anything. You should know my reputation as well." He continued moving, and Spook turned along with him. "I'm stubborn as hell and never do anything I don't want to do. You should have known that before you accepted the job." He kept moving. Bull hoped Zach would see or hear what was going on and hole up in the bedroom until Bull could take care of Spook.

"Yeah, yeah," Spook said. "You think I really care now? All I want is my money, and I'll take what I want out of you or the little piece you have in the bedroom. Either way, I won't be leaving with nothing."

"I'm afraid you will," Bull said. Sirens sounded in the distance.

"Like I said, I don't think so."

Spook raised the gun, and Bull glanced around, trying to figure out his options. Suddenly, Spook went flying, hit the counter, and then crumpled to the floor, Zach a blur of movement from behind him. A shot rang out, and Bull hit the floor as well before lunging toward Spook as he tried to get up. "Kick the gun away," Bull told Zach, who now stood naked in the kitchen doorway. He did as Bull asked and stared at them.

"I called the police," Zach said, breathing hard and shaking a little.

"Good idea. I've got him. I suggest you go put some clothes on," Bull said. Zach looked down, squeaked, and hurried back toward the bedroom.

"What the hell happened?" Spook groaned as Bull held his hands behind his back.

"Doesn't matter, dumbass. But it seems Zach laid you out. The police are on their way, and you can explain to them why you were here and what you thought you were doing, or you can get the hell out of here and forget about me, because if I ever see you again, I'll speak to all of my contacts. You won't be able to get a job doing anything after that. No one will trust you for anything. I might be out of the game, but you know I can make your life difficult. So make your choice—you've got just a few seconds."

"Fine," Spook said. Bull lifted him to his feet, not really caring if Spook was in pain or not. "Get out and gone." Bull opened the door to the backyard and shoved Spook out into the night. He really didn't want to have to explain to the police about his background or about Spook. It was doubtful they'd see Spook again. He'd been beaten, and that was something Spook wouldn't want to get around.

"Where'd he go?" Zach asked as he approached the kitchen in Bull's robe. It looked huge on him.

"He got away," Bull said.

"Uh-huh," Zach said. "I don't think I want to know. Just tell the police what you need to, and I'll nod and say I didn't see anything."

A knock sounded on the door, and Zach hurried to open it. They spent the next little while with the police explaining that they'd heard a noise in the house and had panicked. Zach kept quiet while Bull handled the police and apologized for any inconvenience.

"You lied to them so easily," Zach said once the police were gone.

"Think of it as sort of the mercenary's code." Bull stroked the top of his own head. "My past is shadowy. I operated under different identities, and there are many things I would rather not explain. If they found Spook on my kitchen floor, he and I would both spend a great deal of time trying to avoid questions we can't or shouldn't answer." Bull took Zach's hand. "He won't be back. You scared the crap out of him when you knocked his legs from under him. You realize that's twice in twenty-four hours you've used that move?"

"I wasn't about to let him hurt you," Zach said.

158

"See? You are a superhero," Bull told Zach with a smile.

Zach yawned wide. "I have to be at work in a few hours," he said, placing his hands on his hips. "There aren't going to be other people coming in and having a seat at your kitchen table, are there? We've had a messenger who tried to kill you and a world leader— all we need is a movie star and the menagerie will be complete. Oh, and let's not forget your mother dropping by unannounced."

Bull shuddered. Of all the things Zach had mentioned, his mother's surprise visit had been the biggest shock. "God, I hope not. But I can't guarantee anything, except that my mother has promised to call from now on." He checked the doors, not that the locks seemed to keep anyone out, and turned out the lights before leading Zach back to the bedroom. Bull sat on the edge of the bed and untied the robe Zach had on. "I like you wearing my robe," Bull whispered. "In fact, I think I like you in anything of mine." He parted the fabric and pushed it off Zach's shoulders, then wrapped his arms around Zach's waist, tugged him close, and rested his cheek against Zach's belly. "I don't know how you did it."

"Did what?"

"I always thought I didn't need anyone and that I could survive just fine on my own. But I can't see myself doing anything without you." Bull lightly stroked down Zach's back, then cupped the smooth skin of his butt. "I worry that I'm too old for you and that you'll want someone else once you get tired of me."

Zach stroked over Bull's head and down to his cheeks. "I love you," he whispered. "You're my superhero." He kept going, trailing his hands down Bull's chest and belly before opening his jeans and pushing them down Bull's hips. Bull shuddered, but didn't let Zach distract his thought.

"But what if I can't be?" Bull asked. "I can't live up to some ideal of what you want. I'm just me."

"I know that," Zach said, leaning down to kiss him. "Being yourself is all I ask." Zach pressed forward, and Bull settled back on the bed. Zach undid the robe, and it fell open. Bull closed his eyes as Zach made long, slow strokes up and down his chest. Bull felt like a cat being petted, and damned if that wasn't amazing. Bull's skin tingled as Zach slowly stroked his chest and belly. He held his breath whenever Zach got close to his cock, but Zach seemed intent on teasing him.

Zach stopped and pulled away. The bed shifted, and Bull opened his eyes as Zach climbed on the bed, straddling him. Bull placed his feet on the side rail of the bed, and damned if Zach didn't sit across his hips, rocking his pelvis back and forth, sliding his tight little butt along Bull's dick.

Bull reached forward and closed his hand around Zach's cock, then stroked him as he rocked back and forth. Zach's eyes closed and he moaned softly a few times, especially when Bull tightened his grip. "Bull, this was supposed to be for you."

"When we're together it's always about both of us," Bull countered, gently tugging Zach forward and into a kiss. "I want you for always," Bull whispered. "If you'll have me."

"Duh," Zach responded. "Of course I want you." He lightly tweaked one of Bull's nipples, and Bull arched his back into the sensation. "I want to know everything about you." Zach sat back up and traced the small scar just above Bull's hip. "I want to know where you got this, and the one on your shoulder. I want you to tell me all your stories—good and bad." Bull stroked up Zach's sides and felt him shudder slightly.

Bull shifted back on the bed, taking Zach along with him. Once Bull was comfortable, he sighed slightly. Zach smiled at him and began rolling his hips once again. Bull had no idea how much longer he could take this teasing. Zach was driving him out of his mind. He reached to the nightstand and located a condom by feel. Zach tugged it out of his hand, and Bull watched as he used his teeth to open the package. Zach stilled and moved back, grasping Bull in his hands, then slowly, teasingly, rolled the lubed condom down his length, stroking and playing as he did. Bull throbbed in Zach's hand, trying desperately not to come.

Thankfully, Zach stopped before Bull got to the edge, and Bull blew air out of his lungs, watching Zach as he searched for the lube.

Zach squirted some on his fingers and reached around behind himself. Bull groaned, wanting desperately to watch as Zach's long fingers slid into his tight butt. Bull moaned, and Zach arched his back. Then he moved back, took Bull's cock, and guided it to his opening.

Bull held his breath and remained still as Zach pressed back, slowly taking him into tight heat that made Bull groan with deep joy. Nothing he had ever experienced compared to the soul-calming warmth and care of entering Zach's body. It was more than sex—it reached to his heart and didn't let go. Zach moaned and Bull held still, denying the near-desperate urge to thrust deep and hard. Zach whimpered softly, and Bull moaned along with him as Zach rested his butt on his hips. "Damn, you're hot," Bull groaned.

Zach shifted slightly and then sat. Bull wanted to grab him by the hips and thrust upward until he couldn't see. But he didn't move. Slowly, Zach lifted himself up and then sliding back down onto him. "Stay still," Zach told him.

"Pushy bottom," Bull chided.

"Yeah," Zach said, lifting himself again until Bull nearly pulled out, and then plunging down onto him. "You better believe it, and from the look on your face, you love it." Zach lifted himself then drove down onto Bull again and again. The movements increased in pace until Zach began bouncing off Bull's hips. When Bull could take no more, he began meeting his movements, thrusting upward. Zach placed his hands on Bull's chest while Bull held Zach's sides.

Within minutes, Zach glistened with sweat, and from the panting and gasping, neither of them seemed able to get enough air. "Jesus," Bull swore, thrusting hard upward as skin slapped against skin. Zach arched his back, head hanging back, mouth open, eyes slightly glassy. Bull took control, driving upward as he held Zach still. "Stroke yourself," Bull said. "I want to watch you and feel you come on my cock. Show me what I'm doing to you."

Zach gasped and reached for his cock, then started stroking slowly. "It's too much," he whimpered.

"No, it's not. It's perfect—you're perfect." Bull could barely see straight, and his attention focused solely on Zach. He was in love with the man, completely, totally, world-centered in love with him. Nothing else mattered. Bull felt himself approaching the edge, but he held off. Zach was euphoric, mumbling incoherently, moving on his cock, moving his hand so fast Bull could hardly see it. That sight alone should have been decadent enough to make him come, but he held on. "I love you, Zach. Now come for me. I want to see you, want you to fly for me. I have you and nothing bad will happen, so let go and give in to it."

Zach whimpered, arching his back further. Then he stilled, moaning loudly, his already tight body clenching around Bull. Bull sucked hard for air as Zach came, crying out to the rafters. Bull held still for a few seconds until all instinct protested so loudly he could take it no more. Then he thrust upward, bouncing Zach on his hips until he plunged over the precipice of pleasure.

Bull remembered almost nothing for a long time. All he did was float. As he came back to himself, he opened his eyes. Zach stared back at him. Bull tugged him down and held him tight, kissing him gently.

"I love you so much," Zach told him.

Bull opened his mouth to say the special words in return, but Zach kissed them away. Bull held Zach tight, and words paled in comparison to having Zach in his arms. He turned on his side, taking Zach along with him. When their bodies separated, Zach groaned softly. Bull slowly left the bed and went into the bathroom to clean himself before returning with a cloth. Zach was already half asleep, a small smile on his face. By the time Bull returned from taking care of the cloth, Zach was feeling around the bed, sweeping his arm over the covers. Bull climbed back in the bed, and Zach curled right next to him.

"What?" Bull whispered, not sure Zach had said anything.

"My superhero," Zach mumbled, resting his head against Bull's chest.

162

"You're the superhero," Bull whispered. Zach's eyes were closed, and Bull doubted he'd heard him. But it was still the truth. Zach had saved Bull from a life of loneliness, devoid of camaraderie and love. He'd seen beneath the tough exterior Bull portrayed, and Bull would be forever grateful and vowed in the darkness to always make sure Zach knew just how much he was loved and how much joy he'd brought to his life. Moving slowly, Bull kissed Zach's forehead, and he rolled over. Bull got comfortable, resting his hand on Zach's hip. Within seconds, Zach had clasped it in his own hand and brought it to his chest, placing Bull's hand over his heart.

EPILOGUE

Four months later

BULL WAS standing in his mother's guest room with Zach. Before meeting Zach and the now infamous visit from his mother, Bull would never have thought he would be staying in his mother's guest room with his partner. Hell, he never thought his mother would accept anything but what she was comfortable with. "Boys?" A knock sounded on the door. "You better be decent," his mother said and then pushed the door open. "We need to go in a few minutes if you're going to make it on time."

"Thank you," Zach said quietly, and Bull's mother's expression softened.

"Of course, sweetheart," she said. Zach and his mother had not only learned to get along, but now actually liked each other. When she called the house, she often asked to speak to Zach or just talked to whichever of the two of them answered the phone. "Traffic is really heavy today, so the sooner we can go, the better." She left the room.

"I'm so nervous." Zach turned to him. "Do you think I look okay?"

Bull rolled his eyes. "Yes." He rummaged in his bag, pulled out a T-shirt, and handed it to Zach. "I was going to give you this at the shop, but I think you should have it now." Zach took it and unfolded the fabric.

"Oh my God, it's Bull," Zach squealed and instantly began pulling off his shirt. He shrugged on the T-shirt and threw himself into Bull's arms. "It's perfect."

Bull leaned forward and kissed Zach gently. "I'm glad you like it. I had a dozen made up. I thought you could put them on your table. It will give you something to drive some interest." Bull handed Zach a brown shopping bag. "Now, let's go before we never make it out of this room." He looked longingly at the bed.

Zach giggled and stepped away. "Okay. Go on and make sure your mother is all set. I'll be right out."

Bull grabbed his small canvas bag and found his mother in the living room, getting her purse. Zach joined them a few minutes later, and they left the house. His mother locked the door, and Bull followed her to her car. Zach climbed in the backseat, and Bull rode up front. Once they were buckled in, they began the trek to Mega Comics. Zach had finished his comic book and found a small house to publish it. Bull's mother drove to the freeway, and once she entered the flow of traffic, she turned into a NASCAR driver. She zoomed through traffic, weaving around other cars until she reached her exit. Bull looked over his shoulder and saw Zach hanging on for dear life.

"I'll have you there in just a few minutes," she said, following the GPS instructions and eventually parking in front of the store. "Okay," she said, turning off the engine. Bull shook his head and opened the door, then stepped out into the relative warmth of Tampa in January. "I have some errands to run, but I'll be back in two hours."

"Thank you," Zach said. Bull saw he was still a little wobbly on his feet. His mother's driving could do that to the strongest of men.

She smiled, and Bull checked his watch. They had half an hour before the signing was scheduled to begin. When he and Zach had decided to visit Bull's mom and stepdad, they had contacted the store to see if they could arrange a signing for Zach while they were in town. The store had been gracious and had said they were arranging a signing of independent comics for the same weekend and had worked Zach into their event.

"What if no one is interested?" Zach asked as they walked toward the door. "What if I sit there for two hours and no one talks to me?"

"Then we go home, and when Mom and Mario go out for dinner, I'll make you forget all about it." Bull saw Zach shiver, and he grinned widely. "Now let's go." Bull held out his hand, and Zach took it as they walked the last few feet to the front door together.

They stepped into the store and Bull looked around.

"Zach?" a young man asked.

"That's me," Zach said. Bull detected the nervous excitement in his voice and placed his hand gently against the small of his back.

"I'm Steve, and I'm so excited you're here," he said, shaking Zach's hand.

"This is my partner, Bull. In case you haven't guessed, he's the inspiration for my hero." Zach grinned up at him, and Bull saw Steve's eyes widen for a second.

"We've got three other artists with us today." Steve led him toward one of the tables. "This will be your space. The rest of the guys got here a little while ago. They went to get lunch, but should be back in a few minutes. Go ahead and set up whatever you have. I'll bring out the books, and we'll be ready to get started." Steve hurried away, glancing back at him before leaving the room. Bull and Zach set out the T-shirts and cover graphics the publisher had made for them. Then Zach took a seat behind the table. He looked adorable, and Bull took pictures with his phone while Zach smiled at the camera.

"You don't have to sit around if you don't want to," Zach said, and Bull saw him looking at the gym bag.

"I thought I'd see if there was a gym nearby," Bull said and leaned close. "You're going to be great." He smiled and then headed for the door.

ZACH WAS disappointed Bull had left, but that only lasted a few minutes, until the store began to fill. Then his nerves disappeared and he began having a good time. He also realized Bull would have been bored. He'd sold his first book to a customer, and he had nervously picked up his pen to sign his very first copy when the store door opened and everyone instantly went silent. Zach looked up and his hand stilled.

Bull walked through the door, shirtless, with horns on his head, just like Zach's comic book hero. He looked menacing, hot, and absolutely perfect. Almost instantly, Zach watched as other copies of his book were snatched up and a line formed at the cash register. Bull walked through the store and stood behind him with his arms folded over his strongly muscled, hairy chest.

"Where did you get those?" Zach asked.

"Jeremy had them made for me," Bull said. "I thought I'd surprise you."

"It certainly worked," Zach said. He turned and began signing books. Customers bought the T-shirts as well, and asked both him and Bull to sign them. In less than two hours, they sold all the books, T-shirts, and had then given away cards he'd signed as well to the people who hadn't been able to get a book. It was amazing and beyond his wildest imagination. "I can't believe you did this for me," Zach said, raking his gaze over Bull.

"Of course I did," Bull said pulling off the horns one by one and placing them in his bag. Then he pulled his Bull graphic T-shirt out of the bag and tugged it on. Zach moved a little closer.

"Do you think you could put those on again once we're alone?" Zach asked, conjuring images of Bull in those horns.

"I think we'll need to wait until we're back in our own bed, but yeah. I think I can give you a private performance." Bull pulled him close and hugged him tightly. "In fact, I'll give you as many as you want for the rest of our lives." Bull leaned close and growled softly into his ear.

"I know," Zach said. "I love you too."

ANDREW GREY grew up in western Michigan with a father who loved to tell stories and a mother who loved to read them. Since then he has lived all over the country and traveled throughout the world. He has a master's degree from the University of Wisconsin-Milwaukee and works in information systems for a large corporation. Andrew's hobbies include collecting antiques, gardening, and leaving his dirty dishes anywhere but in the sink (particularly when writing). He considers himself blessed with an accepting family, fantastic friends, and the world's most supportive and loving partner. Andrew currently lives in beautiful historic Carlisle, Pennsylvania.

Visit Andrew's website at http://www.andrewgreybooks.com and blog at http://andrewgreybooks.livejournal.com/.

E-mail him at andrewgrey@comcast.net.

The Art Series from ANDREW GREY

http://www.dreamspinnerpress.com

The Bottled Up Series from ANDREW GREY

http://www.dreamspinnerpress.com

Love Means… Series from ANDREW GREY

http://www.dreamspinnerpress.com

Love Means… Series from ANDREW GREY

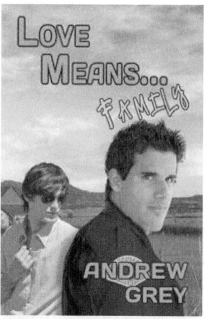

http://www.dreamspinnerpress.com

Taste of Love Stories from ANDREW GREY

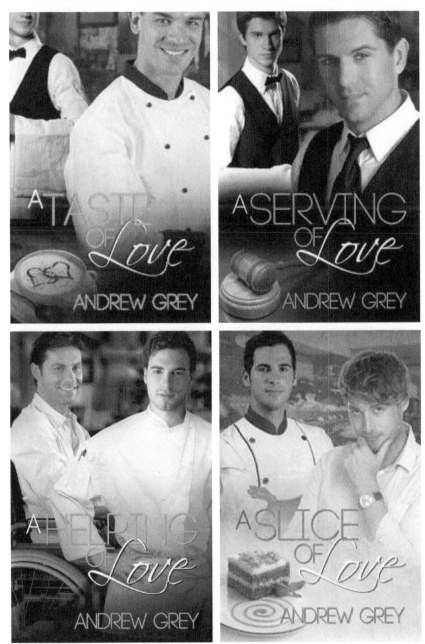

http://www.dreamspinnerpress.com

Children of Bacchus Stories from ANDREW GREY

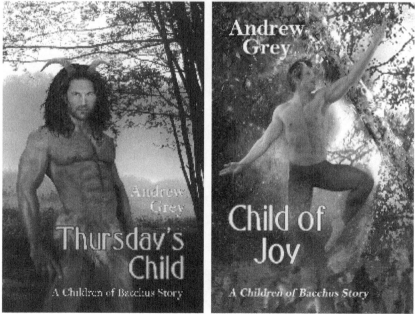

http://www.dreamspinnerpress.com

Good Fight Stories from ANDREW GREY

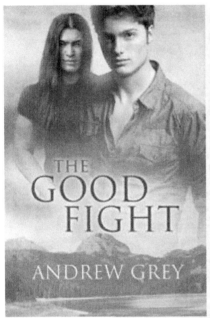

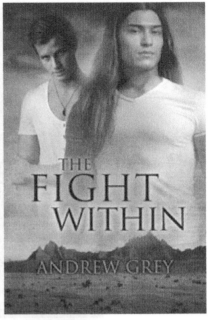

http://www.dreamspinnerpress.com

Stories from the Range from ANDREW GREY

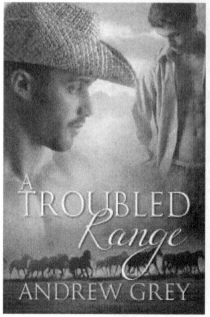

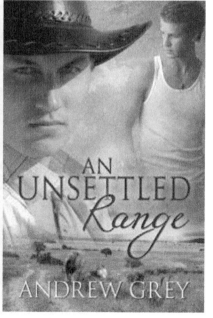

http://www.dreamspinnerpress.com

Stories from the Range from ANDREW GREY

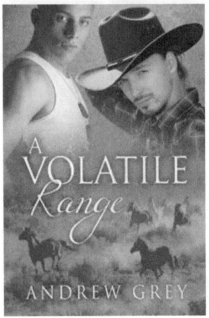

http://www.dreamspinnerpress.com

The Bullriders from ANDREW GREY

http://www.dreamspinnerpress.com

Senses Stories from ANDREW GREY

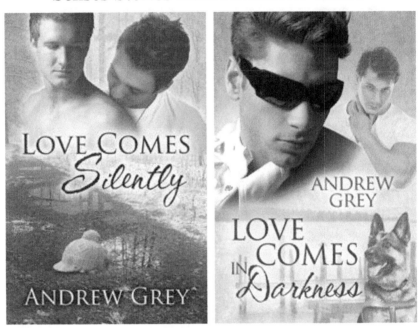

http://www.dreamspinnerpress.com

Seven Days Stories from ANDREW GREY

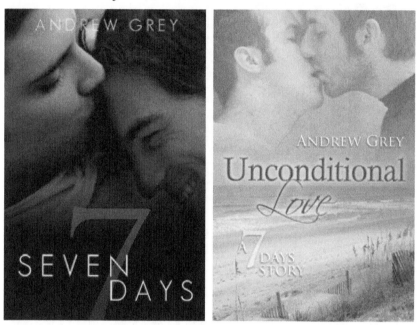

http://www.dreamspinnerpress.com

The Fire Series from ANDREW GREY

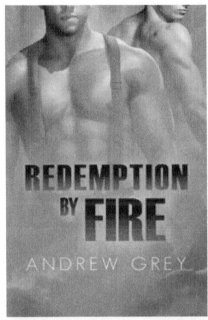

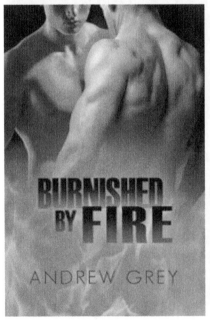
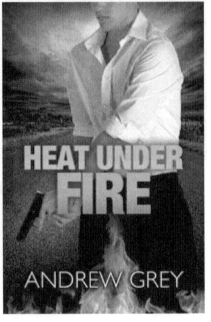

http://www.dreamspinnerpress.com

Work Out Series from ANDREW GREY

http://www.dreamspinnerpress.com

Work Out Series from ANDREW GREY

http://www.dreamspinnerpress.com

Children of Bacchus Stories from ANDREW GREY

 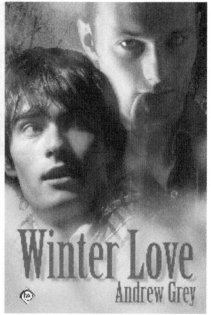

http://www.dreamspinnerpress.com

Also from ANDREW GREY

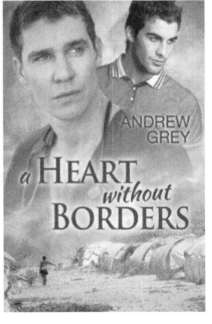

http://www.dreamspinnerpress.com

Also from ANDREW GREY

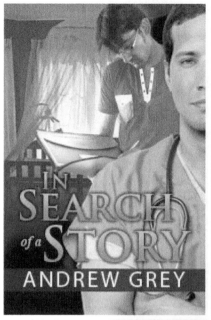

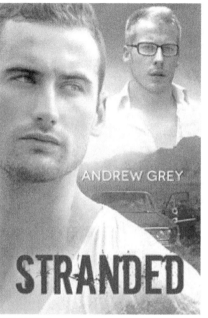

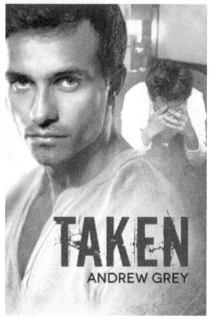

http://www.dreamspinnerpress.com

Novellas from ANDREW GREY

http://www.dreamspinnerpress.com

Novellas from ANDREW GREY

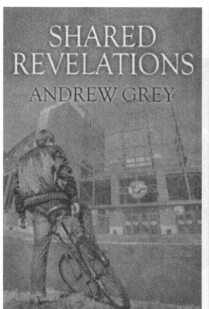

http://www.dreamspinnerpress.com

For more of the
best M/M romance,
visit

Dreamspinner Press

www.dreamspinnerpress.com

CPSIA information can be obtained at www.ICGtesting.com
Printed in the USA
BVOW11s0255270214

346141BV00007B/138/P

9 781627 982627